D0728947

B.J. Daniels is a *New York Times* and *USA TODAY* bestselling author. She wrote her first book after a career as an award-winning newspaper journalist and author of thirty-seven published short stories. She lives in Montana with her husband, Parker, and three springer spaniels. When not writing, she quilts, boats and plays tennis. Contact her at bjdaniels.com, on Facebook or on Twitter, @bjdanielsauthor.

Books by B.J. Daniels

Harlequin Intrigue

Whitehorse, Montana: The McGraw Kidnapping

Dark Horse

Whitehorse, Montana

Secret of Deadman's Coulee
The New Deputy in Town
The Mystery Man of Whitehorse
Classified Christmas
Matchmaking with a Mission
Second Chance Cowboy
Montana Royalty
Shotgun Bride

Visit the Author Profile page at Harlequin.com for more titles.

CAST OF CHARACTERS

Nikki St. James—The true-crime writer is determined to get to the bottom of the famous McGraw twins kidnapping—even if it kills her.

Cull McGraw—The eldest son, the handsome cowboy has a secret about the night of the kidnapping he's been keeping for twenty-five years.

Travers McGraw—With his health failing, he's desperate to find out what happened to his two kidnapped youngest children.

Patricia Owens McGraw—She was the nanny twenty-five years ago when the twins were kidnapped from their beds. Now she's the second Mrs. Travers McGraw.

Marianne McGraw—The mother of the kidnapped twins never recovered and now spends her days in a mental institution.

Frieda Holmes—The McGraw family cook is terrified that her own secrets about the night of the kidnapping will be discovered.

Ledger McGraw—The youngest son was only three, but he might have seen at least one of the kidnappers.

Jim Waters—The family attorney doesn't believe the kidnapped twins will ever be found. At least not alive.

Blake Ryan—The former ranch manager and family friend has his own reasons for hanging around.

Chapter One

Their footfalls echoed among the terrified screams and woeful sobbing as they moved down the long hallway. The nurse's aide, a young woman named Tess, stopped at a room in the criminally insane section of the hospital and, with trembling fingers, pulled out a key to unlock the door.

"I really shouldn't be doing this," Tess said, looking around nervously. As the door swung open, she quickly moved back. Nikki St. James felt a gust of air escape the room like an exhaled breath. The light within the interior was dim, but she could hear the sound of a chair creaking rhythmically.

"I'm going to have to lock the door behind you," Tess whispered.

"Not yet." It took a moment for Nikki's eyes to adjust to the dim light within the room. She fought back the chill that skittered over her skin like spider legs as her gaze finally lit on the occupant.

"This is the wrong one," Nikki said, and tried to step back into the hallway.

"That's her," the nurse's aide said, keeping her voice down. "That's Marianne McGraw."

Nikki stared at the white-haired, slack-faced woman rocking back and forth, back and forth, her gaze blank as if blind. "That woman is too old. Her hair—"

"Her hair turned white overnight after...well, after what happened. She's been like this ever since." Tess shuddered and hugged herself as if she felt the same chill Nikki did.

"She hasn't spoken in all that time?"

"Not a word. Her husband comes every day to visit her. She never responds."

Nikki was surprised that Travers McGraw would come to visit his former wife at all, given what she was suspected of doing. Maybe, like Nikki, he came hoping for answers. "What about her children?"

"They visit occasionally, the oldest son more than the others, but she doesn't react as if she knows any of them. That's all she does, rock like that for hours on end."

Cull McGraw, the oldest son, Nikki thought. He'd been seven, a few years older than her, at the time of the kidnapping. His brothers Boone and Ledger were probably too young to remember the kidnapping, maybe even too young to really remember their mother.

"If you're going in, you'd best hurry," Tess said, still looking around nervously.

Nikki took a step into the room, hating the thought of the nurse's aide locking the door behind her. As her eyes adjusted more to the lack of light, she saw that the woman had something clutched against her chest. A chill snaked up her spine as she made out two small glassy-eyed faces looking out at her from under matted heads of blond hair.

"What's that she's holding?" she whispered hoarsely as she hurriedly turned to Tess before the woman could close and lock the door.

"Her babies."

"Her *babies*?"

"They're just old dolls. They need to be thrown in the trash. We tried to switch them with new ones, but she had a fit. When we bathe or change her, we have to take them away. She screams and tears at her hair until we give them back. It was the doctor's idea, giving her the dolls. Before that, she was…violent. She had to be sedated or you couldn't get near her. Like I said, you go in there at your own risk. She's… unpredictable and if provoked, dangerous since she's a lot stronger than she looks. If I were you, I'd make it quick."

Nikki reached for her notebook as the door closed behind her. The tumblers in the lock sounded like a cannon going off as Tess locked the door.

At your own risk. Comforting words, Nikki thought as she took a tentative step deeper into the padded room. She'd read everything she could find on the McGraw kidnapping case. There'd been a lot of media coverage at the time—and a lot of speculation. Every anniversary for years, the same information had been repeated along with the same plea for anything about the two missing twins, Oakley Travers McGraw and Jesse Rose McGraw.

But no one had ever come forward. The ransom money had never been recovered nor the babies found. There'd been nothing new to report at the one-year anniversary, then the five, ten, fifteen and twenty year.

Now with the twenty-fifth one coming up, few people other than those around Whitehorse, Montana, would probably even remember the kidnapping.

"There is nothing worse than old news," her grandfather had told her when she'd dropped by his office at the large newspaper where he was publisher. Wendell St. James had been sitting behind his huge desk, his head of thick gray hair as wild as his eyebrows, his wire-rimmed glasses perched precariously on his patrician nose. "You're wasting your time with this one."

Actually he thought she was wasting her time writing true crime books. He'd hoped that she would follow him into the newspaper business instead. It didn't matter that out of the nine books she'd written, she'd solved seven of the crimes.

"*Someone* knows what happened that night," she'd argued.

"Well, if they do, it's a pretty safe bet they aren't going to suddenly talk after twenty-five years."

"Maybe they're getting old and they can't live with what they've done," she'd said. "It wouldn't be the first time."

He'd snorted and settled his steely gaze on her. "I wasn't for the other stories you chased, but this one…" He shook his head. "Don't you think I know what you're up to? I suspect this is your mother's fault. She just couldn't keep her mouth shut, could she?"

"She didn't tell me about my father," she'd corrected her grandfather. "I discovered it on my own." For years, she'd believed she was the daughter of a stranger her mother had fallen for one night. A mistake. "All these years, the two of you have lied to me, letting me believe I was an accident, a one-night stand and that explained why I had my mother's maiden name."

"We protected you, you mean. And now you've got some lamebrained idea of clearing your father's name." Wendell swore under his breath. "My daughter has proven that she is the worst possible judge of men, given her track record. But I thought you were smarter than this."

"There was no real proof my father was involved," Nikki had argued stubbornly. Her biological father had been working at the Sundown Stallion Station the summer of the kidnapping. His name had been linked with Marianne McGraw's, the mother of the twins. "Mother doesn't believe he had an affair with Marianne, nor does she believe he had any part in the kidnapping."

"What do you expect your mother to say?" he'd demanded.

"She knew him better than you."

Her grandfather mugged a disbelieving face. "What else did she tell you about the kidnapping?"

Her mother had actually known little. While Nikki would have demanded answers, her mother said she was just happy to visit with her husband, since he was locked up until his trial.

"She didn't ask him anything about the kidnapping because your mother wouldn't have wanted to hear the truth."

She'd realized then that her grandfather's journalistic instincts had clearly skipped a generation. Nikki would have had to know everything about that night, even if it meant finding out that her husband was involved.

"A jury of twelve found him guilty of not only the affair—but the kidnapping," her grandfather had said.

"On circumstantial evidence."

"On the testimony of the nanny who said that Marianne McGraw wasn't just unstable, she feared she might hurt the twins. The nanny also testified that she saw Marianne with your father numerous times in the barn and they seemed…close."

She'd realized that her grandfather knew more about this case than he'd originally let on. "Yes, the nanny, the woman who is now the new wife of Travers McGraw. That alone is suspicious. I would think you'd encourage me to get the real story of what happened that night. And what does…*close* mean anyway?"

Her grandfather had put down his pen with an impatient sigh. "The case is dead cold after twenty-five years. Dozens of very good reporters, not to mention FBI agents and local law enforcement, did their best to solve it, so what in hell's name makes you think that you can find something that they missed?"

She'd shrugged. "I have my grandfather's stubborn arrogance and the genes of one of the suspects. Why not me?"

He'd wagged his gray head again. "Because you're too personally involved, which means that whatever story you get won't be worth printing."

She'd dug her heels in. "I became a true crime writer because I wanted to know more than what I read in the newspapers."

"Bite your tongue," her grandfather said, only half joking. He sobered then, looking worried. "What if you don't like what you find out about your father, or your mother, for that matter? I know my daughter."

"What does that mean?"

He gave another shake of his gray head. "Clearly your mind is made up and since I can't sanction this…" With an air of dismissal, he picked up his pen again. "If that's all…"

She started toward the door but before she could exit, he called after her, "Watch your back, Punky." It had been his nickname for her since she was a baby. "Remember what I told you about family secrets."

People will kill to keep them, she thought now as she looked at Marianne McGraw.

The woman's rocking didn't change as Nikki stepped deeper into the room. "Mrs. McGraw?" She glanced behind her. The nurse's aide stood just outside the door, glancing at her watch.

Nikki knew she didn't have much time. It hadn't been easy getting in here. It had cost her fifty bucks after she'd found the nurse's aide was quitting soon to get married. She would have paid a lot more since so few people had laid eyes on Marianne McGraw in years.

She reached in her large purse for the camera she'd brought. No reporter had gotten in to see Marianne McGraw. Nikki had seen a photograph of Marianne McGraw taken twenty-five years ago, before her infant fraternal twins, a boy and girl, had been kidnapped. She'd been a beauty at thirty-two, a gorgeous dark-haired woman with huge green eyes and a contagious smile.

That woman held no resemblance to the one in the rocking chair. Marianne was a shell of her former self, appearing closer to eighty than fifty-seven.

"Mrs. McGraw, I'm Nikki St. James. I'm a true crime writer. How are you doing today?"

Nikki was close enough now that she could see nothing but blankness in the woman's green-eyed stare. It was as if Marianne McGraw had gone blind—and deaf, as well. The face beneath the wild mane of white hair was haggard, pale, lifeless. The mouth hung open, the lips cracked and dry.

"I want to ask you about your babies," Nikki said. "Oakley and Jesse Rose?" Was it her imagination or did the woman clutch the dolls even harder to her thin chest?

"What happened the night they disappeared?" Did Nikki really expect an answer? She could hope, couldn't she? Mostly, she needed to hear the sound of her voice in this claustrophobic room. The rocking had a hypnotic effect, like being pulled down a rabbit hole.

"Everyone outside this room believes you had something to do with it. You and Nate Corwin." No response, no reaction to the name. "Was he your lover?"

She moved closer, catching the decaying scent that rose from the rocking chair as if the woman was already dead. "I don't believe it's true. But I think you might know who kidnapped your babies," she whispered.

The speculation at the time was that the kidnapping had been an inside job. Marianne had been suffering from postpartum depression. The nanny had said that Mrs. McGraw was having trouble bonding with the babies and that she'd been afraid to leave Marianne alone with them.

And, of course, there'd been Marianne's secret lover—the man who everyone believed had helped her kidnap her own children. He'd been implicated because of a shovel found in the stables with his bloody fingerprints on it—along with fresh soil—even though no fresh graves had been found.

"Was Nate Corwin involved, Marianne?" The court had decided that Marianne McGraw couldn't have acted alone. To get both babies out the second-story window, she would have needed an accomplice.

"Did my father help you?"

There was no sign that the woman even heard her, let alone recognized her alleged lover's name. And if the woman *had* answered, Nikki knew she would have jumped out of her skin.

She checked to make sure Tess wasn't watching as she snapped a photo of the woman in the rocker. The flash lit the room for an instant and made a *snap* sound. As she started to take another, she thought she heard a low growling sound coming from the rocker.

She hurriedly took another photo, though hesitantly, as the growling sound seemed to grow louder. Her eye on the viewfinder, she was still focused on the woman in the rocker when Marianne McGraw seemed to rock forward as if lurching from her chair.

A shriek escaped her before she could pull

down the camera. She had closed her eyes and thrown herself back, slamming into the wall. Pain raced up one shoulder. She stifled a scream as she waited for the feel of the woman's claw-like fingers on her throat.

But Marianne McGraw hadn't moved. It had only been a trick of the light. And yet, Nikki noticed something different about the woman.

Marianne was smiling.

Chapter Two

When a hand touched her shoulder, Nikki jumped, unable to hold back the cry of fright.

"We have to go," Tess said, tugging on her shoulder. "They'll be coming around with meds soon."

Nikki hadn't heard the nurse's aide enter the room. Her gaze had been on Marianne McGraw—until Tess touched her shoulder.

Now she let her gaze go back to the woman. The white-haired patient was hunched in her chair, rocking back and forth, back and forth. The only sound in the room was that of the creaking rocking chair and the pounding of Nikki's pulse in her ears.

Marianne's face was slack again, her mouth open, the smile gone. If it had ever been there.

Nikki tried to swallow the lump in her throat. She'd let her imagination get the best of her, thinking that the woman had risen up from that rocker for a moment.

But she hadn't imagined the growling sound any more than she would forget that smile of amusement. Marianne McGraw was still inside that shriveled-up old white-haired woman.

And if she was right, she thought, looking down at the camera in her hand, there would be proof in the photos she'd taken.

Tess pulled on her arm. "You have to go. *Now.* And put that camera away!"

Nikki nodded and let Tess leave the room ahead of her. All her instincts told her to get out now. She'd read that psychopaths were surprisingly strong and with only Tess to pull the woman off her...

She studied the white-haired woman in the rocker, trying to decide if Marianne McGraw was the monster everyone believed her to be.

"Did you let Nate Corwin die for a crime he didn't commit?" Nikki whispered. "Is your real accomplice still out there, spending the $250,000 without you? Or are you innocent in all this? As innocent as I believe my father was?"

For just an instant she thought she saw something flicker in Marianne McGraw's green eyes. The chill that climbed up her backbone froze her to her core. "You *know* what happened that night, don't you," Nikki whispered at the woman. In frustration, she realized that if her father and this woman were behind the kidnaping, Marianne might be the *only* person alive who knew the truth.

"Come on!" Tess whispered from the hallway.

Nikki was still staring at the woman in the rocker. "I'm going to find out." She turned to leave. Behind her, she heard the chilling low growling sound emanating from Marianne Mc-Graw. It wasn't until the door was closed and locked behind her that she let out the breath she'd been holding.

TESS MOTIONED FOR Nikki to follow her. The hallway was long and full of shadows this late at night. Their footfalls sounded too loud on the linoleum floor. The air was choked with the smell of disinfectants that didn't quite cover the…other smells.

Someone cried out in a nearby room, making Nikki start. Behind them there were moans broken occasionally by bloodcurdling screams. She almost ran the last few feet to the back door.

Tess turned off the alarm, pushed open the door and, checking to make sure she had her keys, stepped out into the night air with her. They both breathed in the Montana night. Stars glittered in the midnight blue of the big sky overhead. In the distance, she could make out the dark outline of the Little Rockies.

"I told you she wouldn't be any help to your story," Tess said after a moment.

Nikki could tell that the nurse's aide couldn't wait until her last day at this job. She could see how a place like that would wear on you. Though she'd spent little time inside, she still was having trouble shaking it off.

"I still appreciate you letting me see her." She knew the only reason she'd gotten in was because the nurse's aide was getting married, had already given her two weeks' notice and was planning to move to Missoula with her future husband. Nikki had read it in the local newspaper under Engagements. It was why she'd made a point of finding out when Tess worked her last late-night shifts.

Nearby an owl hooted. Tess hugged herself even though the night wasn't that cold. Nikki longed for any sound other than the creak of a rocking chair. She feared she would hear it in her sleep.

"I heard you tell her that you were going to find out what happened that night," Tess said. "Everyone around here already knows what happened."

Did they? Nikki thought of Marianne Mc-Graw. Her hair had turned white overnight and now she was almost a corpse. The only man who might know whether the rumors were true, Nikki's own father, was dead.

"What does everyone believe happened?" she asked.

"She was having an affair with her horse trainer, so of course that's who she got to help her get rid of the babies," Tess said as she dug in her pocket for a cigarette. "I'm trying to quit. Before the wedding. But some nights…"

Nikki watched her light up and take a long drag. "Wait, why get rid of the babies? She still had three other sons."

"I guess she figured they'd be fine with their father. But babies… Also they needed the money. Easier to kidnap a couple of babies than one of the younger boys who'd make a fuss."

"Still, they didn't have to kill them."

"The horse trainer probably didn't want to be saddled with two babies. Not very romantic running away together with the money—and two squalling babies."

That was the story the prosecution had told that had gotten her father sent to prison. But was it true? "I thought he swore he didn't do it."

She scoffed. "That's what they all say."

Nate Corwin, according to what Nikki had been able to find, had said right up to the end when they were driving him to prison that he didn't do it. Maybe, if the van hadn't overturned and he wasn't killed, then maybe he could have fought his conviction, found proof... Or maybe he'd lied right up until his last breath.

"But I thought it was never proven that he was even Marianne's lover, let alone that he helped her kidnap her own children?" Nikki asked.

The nurse's aide made a disbelieving sound. "Who else was there?"

"I'd heard the nanny might have been involved."

"*Patty?* Well, I wouldn't put it past her."

This caught Nikki's attention. "You know her?"

The nurse's aide pursed her lips as if she shouldn't be talking about this, but fortunately that didn't stop her. Anyway, she'd already broken worse rules today by sneaking Nikki into the hospital.

"She accompanies her husband most of the time. You can tell *Patty* doesn't like him visiting his ex-wife," Tess said. Nikki got the impression that Patricia McGraw also didn't like being called Patty.

"She won't even step into Marianne's room," the nurse's aide was saying between puffs. "Not that I blame her, but instead she stands in the hallway and watches them like a hawk. Imagine being jealous of that poor woman in that room."

"I also heard that Travers McGraw himself might have been involved," Nikki threw out.

Tess shook her head emphatically. "No way. Mr. McGraw is the nicest, kindest man. He would never hurt a fly, let alone his own children." She lowered her voice conspiratorially even though they were alone at the back of the hospital and there was only open country behind them. "He hardly ever leaves the ranch except to come here to see his now ex-wife—that is until recently. I heard he's not feeling well."

Nikki had heard the same thing. Maybe that was why he'd agreed to let her interview him and his family for the book.

When Nikki had first approached him, she had expected him to turn her down in a letter. The fact that she'd made a name for herself after solving the murders in so many of her books had helped, she was sure.

"You seem to have a talent for finding out the truth," Travers McGraw had said when he'd called her out of the blue. He'd been one of just three people she'd contacted about interviews and a book, but he'd been the one she wanted badly.

That was one reason she'd tried not to sound too eager when she'd talked to him. McGraw hadn't done any interviews other than the local press—not since a reporter had broken into his house and scared his family half to death.

"I work at finding the truth," she'd told him, surprised how nervous she was just to hear his voice.

"And you think you can find out the truth in our…case?"

"I want to." More than he could possibly know. "But I should warn you up front, I need access to everyone involved. It would require me basically moving in for a while. Are you sure you're agreeable to that?"

She'd held her breath. Long ago she'd found that making demands made her come off as more professional. It also shifted the power structure. She wasn't begging to do their story. She was doing them a favor.

The long silence on the other end of the line had made her close her eyes, tightening her hand around the phone. She had wanted this so badly. Probably too badly. Maybe she should have—

"When are you thinking of coming here?" Travers McGraw asked.

Her heart had been beating so hard she could barely speak. "I'm finishing up a project now."

"You do realize it's been twenty-five years?"

Not quite. She'd still had two weeks before the actual date that the two babies had been stolen out of the nursery and never seen again. She wanted to be in the house on anniversary night.

"I can be there in a week." She'd crossed her fingers even though she'd never been superstitious.

"I'll take care of everything. Will you be flying to Billings? I can have one of my sons—"

"That won't be necessary. I'll be driving." Though she was anxious to meet his sons. But the only other way, besides driving to Whitehorse, was to take the train that came right through town.

"I hope you can work your magic for us," McGraw said. "If there is anything I can do to help…"

"We'll talk when I get there. It would be best if no one knew I was coming. I'm sure in a small town like Whitehorse, word will get out soon enough."

"Yes, of course."

She'd left a few days before she'd told him she would be arriving. She'd wanted to see Marianne McGraw and get a feel for Whitehorse before she went out to the ranch. Once word got out about her, she would lose her anonymity.

Tess put out her cigarette in the dirt.

"If Travers McGraw is so devoted to the mother of his children, then why did he marry the nanny not long after his divorce?" Nikki asked, hoping to get more out of Tess before she went back inside.

"It was *nine* years after the kidnapping. I heard Patty showed up with a baby in her arms and a sob story. He's a nice man so I guess he was taken in by it." Tess definitely didn't like Patricia McGraw.

"A baby? *Was it his?*"

Again Tess shook her head stubbornly. "He adored his wife Marianne. He still does. Who knows whose baby Patty brought back with her."

"So what are the chances that nanny Patty had something to do with the kidnapping?"

Tess raised an eyebrow as she looked anxiously toward the back door of the hospital. "She got the husband, didn't she? Everyone says she married him for his money since there's a pretty big difference in their ages and she wouldn't have wanted Marianne's babies to raise. She has her hands full with her own child. Talk about a spoiled brat."

Nikki wondered what had brought the nanny back to the ranch after almost ten years. What if Patty Owens knew something about the kidnapping and Travers McGraw had married her to keep her quiet? But then why wait all those years?

"It certainly does make you wonder, huh,"

Tess said as she reached for the hospital keys. But she hesitated before she opened the door. "Something horrible had to have happened that night to turn her hair white. Something so horrible she can't speak."

"Something other than having her babies kidnapped?" Nikki asked.

Tess shuddered. "I try not to think about it. But if she was in love with the horse trainer…" She leaned toward Nikki and said conspiratorially, "What if she killed the babies before she dropped them out the window?"

Nikki felt a chill race through her. That was something she'd never considered. From what she'd read about the case, it was believed that someone—Marianne, according to the prosecutor—had given the babies cough syrup containing codeine so they would be quiet. Maybe she'd given them too much.

Her head ached. She'd thought of little else but this case since she'd stumbled across the old newspaper clippings in her mother's trunk and learned about her father, Nate Corwin—and the McGraw kidnapping.

At first she hadn't understood why her mother would have kept the stories. That was until she recognized the man in the photograph. The photo of him had been taken on the day Nate Corwin was convicted.

"I always wondered why if you loved my father, you didn't keep the Corwin name since you were legally married, right?" she'd asked her mother, and had seen horror cross her features.

"Why would you ask—" Her mother had never remarried but had gone back to her maiden name, St. James.

"You told me my father died."

"He *did* die."

"You just failed to mention he died on the way to prison for kidnapping and murder."

"He didn't do it. He swore he didn't do it," her mother had cried. She was convinced that her husband hadn't been involved with Marianne McGraw nor had anything to do with the kidnapping, let alone the double murder of two innocent babies.

But *someone* had. And if not her father, then someone had let him be convicted and die for a crime he hadn't committed.

Nikki was determined to get to the truth no matter what it took. She had just short of a week before the twenty-fifth anniversary of the kidnapping to get the real story. Travers desperately wanted her to do the book. It was the family she was worried about.

She'd been thinking about how to get close to at least one of the sons before she headed for

Sundown Stallion Station and met the rest of the McGraws.

If there was one thing she believed it was that the people in that house had more information than they'd given the sheriff twenty-five years ago. They just might not realize the importance of what they'd seen or heard. Or they had their reasons for keeping it to themselves.

"So how did you get into writing crime books?" the nurse's aide asked as if putting off going back down that long hallway by herself.

"It's in my blood," Nikki said. "My grandfather was a Pulitzer Prize–winning newspaper reporter. From as far back as I can remember, I wanted to be just like him."

"He must be proud of you," Tess said almost wistfully.

Nikki nodded distractedly. Proving herself to her grandfather was another reason she would do whatever it took to get the real kidnapping story—or die trying.

Chapter Three

Cull McGraw put down the windows on his pickup as he drove into Whitehorse. It was one of the big sky days where the deep blue ran from horizon to horizon without a cloud. In the distance, snow still capped the top of the Little Rockies, and everywhere he looked he saw spring as the land began to turn green.

Days like this, Cull felt like he could breathe. Part of it was getting out of the house. He just felt lucky that he'd intercepted the newspaper before Frieda, the family cook, had delivered it on the way to the kitchen.

He didn't need a calendar to know what time of the year it was. He had seen the approaching anniversary of the kidnapping in the pained look in his father's eyes. He could feel it take over the main house as if draping it in a black funeral shroud.

Every year, he just rode it out. The day would

pass. Nothing would happen. No one would come forward with information about the missing twins. Another year would pass. Another year of watching his father get his hopes up only to be crushed under the weight of disappointment.

What always made it worse was the age-progression photographs in the newspaper of what Oakley and Jesse Rose would look like now and his father's plea for any information on them.

Ahead, he could see the outskirts of the small Western town. Cull sighed. He should have known there would be a big write-up in the paper, since this would be the twenty-fifth anniversary. He glanced over at the newspaper lying on the seat next to him. He'd read just enough to set him off. When would his father realize that the twins were gone and would never be coming back? Knowing Travers McGraw the way he did, Cull knew his father would hold out hope until his last dying breath.

But this year, the publisher of the paper had talked his younger brother Ledger into an interview. As he drove down the main drag, he spotted Ledger's pickup right where he knew it would be—in front of the Whitehorse Café.

JUST AS NIKKI had done for the past few days, she watched Ledger McGraw enter the Whitehorse Café. He had arrived at the same time each morning, pulled up out front in a Sundown Stallion Station pickup and adjusted his Stetson before climbing out.

Across the street in the park, Nikki observed him from behind the latest weekly newspaper as he hesitated just inside the café door. She saw him looking around, and after watching him for three mornings, she knew exactly what he was looking for. *Who* he was looking for.

He tipped his hat to the young redheaded waitress, just as he had the past three mornings, before he took a seat at a booth in her section. He had been three when the twins were kidnapped, which now made him about twenty-eight. There was an innocence about him and an old-fashioned chivalrous politeness. She'd seen it in the way he wiped his boots on the mat just outside the café door. In the way he always removed his hat the moment he stepped in. In the way he waited to be offered a seat as if he had all day.

She'd keyed in on Ledger when she'd realized that no one else in the McGraw family had such a predictable routine. That wasn't the only reason she'd chosen him. In the days she'd been in town watching him each morning, she had seen his trusting nature and hoped he would be the son she might get to help her.

Nikki didn't kid herself that this was going to be easy. She'd heard from other journalists that the family hated reporters and all of them except Travers had refused to talk about the kidnapping. She desperately needed someone on that ranch who would be agreeable to help her. Ledger might be the one.

Nikki wished she had more time before making her move. But the clock was ticking. The twenty-fifth anniversary of the kidnapping was approaching rapidly. It still gave her a chill when she looked at the photographs she'd taken of Marianne McGraw. It hadn't been her imagination. The woman had risen up from her chair, eyes wild, hands clenched around the "babies" in her arms.

If Nikki had had any doubt that the woman was still in that shell of a body, she no longer did. Now she had to find out if the rumors were true about Marianne and Nate Corwin.

From across the street, she watched Ledger take a seat in his usual booth. A moment later, the redhead put a cup of coffee, a menu and the folded edition of what Nikki assumed was the *Milk River Courier* on his table.

The local weekly had just come out this morning. Ledger had been interviewed, which surprised her, since it was the first time she knew of that he'd spoken to the press, but it also made her even more convinced that Ledger was her way into the family.

Inside the café, she watched Ledger looking bashful as he picked up the menu, but he didn't look at it. Instead, he secretly watched the red-headed waitress as she walked away.

Nikki saw something in his expression that touched her heart. A vulnerability that made her turn away for a moment. There was a yearning that was all too evident to anyone watching.

But no one else *was* watching. Clearly this young man was besotted with this redhead. Today, though, Nikki noticed something she'd missed the days before.

As she watched the waitress return to the table to take his order, she saw *why* she'd missed it. Along with the obvious sexual tension between them, there was the glint of a gold band on the young woman's left-hand ring finger.

Her heart ached all the more for Ledger because this was clearly a case of unrequited love. Add to that an obvious shared history and Nikki knew she was witnessing heartbreak at its rawest. The redhead had moved on, but Ledger apparently hadn't.

High school sweethearts? But if so, what had torn them apart? she wondered, then quickly brushed her curiosity aside. Her grandfather had often warned her about getting emotionally involved with the people she wrote about.

She knew in this case, she had to be especially careful.

"Care, and you lose your objectivity," he'd said when, as a girl, she'd asked how he could write about the pain and suffering of people the way he did. "The best stories are about another person's pain. It's the nature of the business because people who've lost something make good human-interest stories. Everyone can relate because we have all lost something dear to us."

"What have *you* lost?" she'd asked her grandfather, since she'd never seen vulnerability in him ever.

"Nothing."

She'd always assumed that was true. Nothing stopped her grandfather from getting what he wanted. He'd go to any extreme to get a story and later to run the newspaper he bought, even if it meant risking his life or his business. But then again, that was one of the reasons Nikki suspected her grandmother had left him to marry another man. Not that her grandfather had seemed to notice. Or maybe he hid his pain well.

Ledger McGraw was in pain and it couldn't help but touch her heart. Nikki knew her grandfather would encourage her to use this new information to her advantage.

"Keep your eye on the goal," he'd always said. "The goal is getting the best story you possibly can. You aren't there to try to make things better or bond with these people."

That had sounded cold to her.

"It's all about emotional distance. Pretend you're a fly on the wall," he'd said. "A fly that sometimes has to buzz around and get things going if you hope to get anything worth writing about."

Nikki now felt anxious. She had to make her move today. Ledger would be finishing his breakfast soon. She couldn't put this off any longer. Just as she decided it was time, she saw Ledger grab the redhead's wrist as she started to step past his table.

Nikki saw those too shallowly buried emotions arc between them as the waitress reacted to whatever he was saying to her. The waitress jerked free of his hold and looked as if she might cry. But Nikki's gaze was on Ledger's face. His pain was so naked that she couldn't help feeling it at heart level.

Ledger McGraw was incredibly young, his protectiveness for this woman touching. *He's still a boy*, Nikki thought, and felt guilty for what she was about to do.

LEDGER IMMEDIATELY REGRETTED grabbing Abby's wrist. Without looking at her, he said, "He's hurt you again."

"Don't, Ledger."

As she jerked free of his hold, he raised his gaze to meet hers again. "Abby." The word came out a plea. "Any man who would hurt you—"

"Stay out of it, please," she whispered, tears in her eyes. *"Please."* Her lowered voice cracked with emotion. "You don't understand."

He shook his head. He understood only too well. "A man who hurts you doesn't love you."

Her throat worked as she hastily brushed at her tears. "You don't know anything about it," she snapped before rushing toward the kitchen and away from him. "He just grabbed my wrist too hard. It's nothing."

He swore under his breath, realizing he didn't know anything about it. He'd never understood what she saw in Wade Pierce. He especially didn't understand why Abby stayed with the man.

Ledger finished what he could eat of his breakfast. Digging out the cost of his meal and tip from his jeans' pocket, he dropped the money on the table, grabbed his hat and left.

Once outside, he stopped in the bright sunlight as he tried to control the emotions roiling inside him. It wasn't the first time he'd seen the bruises, even though Abby had done her best to hide them. The bastard was mistreating her—he was sure of it.

He wanted to kill Wade with his bare hands. It was all he could do not to drive over to the feedlot and call the man out. But he knew that the only thing that would accomplish was more pain for Abby.

When was she going to see Wade for what he really was—a bully and a blowhard and… With a curse, he realized that Abby might never come to her senses. She was convinced he couldn't live without her.

"Ledger?"

He turned at the sound of a woman's voice.

Marta, the other waitress and a friend of Abby's, held out the newspaper to him. "You forgot this," she said, sympathy in her expression.

That was the trouble with a small town. Everyone knew your business, including watching your heart break. He hadn't looked at the newspaper, wasn't sure he wanted to. He hadn't been thinking when the publisher had cornered him.

He took the paper from Marta and mumbled, "Thanks," before the door closed. Gripping the newsprint, he turned toward his ranch pickup. He felt light-headed with fury and frustration and that constant ache in his heart. Not to mention he was worried about what would happen when the rest of the family saw the story in the paper.

And yet, all he could think about was driving over to the feedlot and dragging Wade out and kicking his butt all the way from Whitehorse to the North Dakota border.

But even as he thought it, he knew he was to blame for this. He'd let Abby get away. He'd practically propelled her into Wade's arms. He hadn't been ready for marriage. As much as he loved her, he'd wanted to wait until he had the money for a place of his own. He couldn't bring Abby into the house at Sundown Stallion Station. He could barely stand living on the ranch himself. He'd told himself he couldn't do that to her. Then Wade had come along, seeming to offer everything Ledger couldn't.

Head down, he was almost to his pickup when he heard someone call his name.

THE COWBOY WHO got out of the second Sundown Stallion Station pickup made Nikki catch her breath. She'd seen photos of Cull McGraw, usually candid paparazzi shots over the years, but none of them captured the raw power of the man in person.

From his broad shoulders to the long denim-clad legs now striding toward his brother, he looked like a man to be reckoned with. The one thing he had in common with all the photos she'd ever seen of him was the scowl.

"Ledger!" Cull looked like he wanted to tear up the pavement as he closed in on his brother. "Have you seen this?" he demanded, waving what appeared to be a newspaper clutched in his big fist.

Ledger stared at him as if confused, as if he was still thinking of the waitress back in the café. Clearly, he hadn't bothered to look at the newspaper he was now gripping in his own hand.

"Why in the hell did you talk to the press? Not to mention, why you didn't tell me that Dad had raised the reward. *Again!*" Cull slapped the paper against his muscular thigh. "Patricia is going to lose her mind over this. All hell is going to break loose."

"We probably shouldn't talk about this out here," she heard Ledger say. "Enough of our lives is open to public consumption, don't you think?"

Cull swore and looked toward the café. Two waitresses stood looking out the large plate-glass window along with several patrons.

"Fine. We'll take this up at home," Cull said through gritted teeth as he turned on his boot heel and headed back toward his pickup.

With an expression of resignation, Ledger turned toward the café window. The redheaded waitress was no longer at the window. He stood for a moment, looking as if he had the weight of the world on his shoulders before he headed for his truck and climbed behind the wheel. The engine revved and he roared past, sending up dust from Whitehorse's main street.

Nikki shifted her gaze to Cull, realizing her plan had just taken a turn she hadn't expected. She hesitated, no longer sure.

Cull had reached his truck, but hadn't gotten in. He was watching Ledger leave, still looking angry.

If Cull was this upset about the article in the newspaper and new reward, wait until he found out that she would be doing a book about the family and the kidnapping case.

She almost changed her mind about the truly dangerous part of her plan. Almost.

JERKING THE DOOR of his pickup open, Cull climbed in, angry with himself for coming here this morning to confront his brother. He should have waited, but he'd been so angry with his brother… He knew Ledger hadn't meant any harm.

Tossing the newspaper on the pickup seat, he reached for the key in the ignition. Like most people in Whitehorse, he'd left his keys in his rig while he'd confronted his brother. Had it been winter instead of a warm spring day, he would have left the truck running so it would be warm when he came back.

The newspaper fell open to the front-page story. A bold two-deck headline ran across the top of the page. Twenty-Five Years After Kidnapping: Where Are the McGraw Twins?

The damned anniversary of the kidnapping was something he dreaded, he thought with a shake of his head. Like clockwork, the paper did a story, longer ones on some years like this one. He hadn't seen anything but the first few quotes, one from his brother Ledger and the other from their father, when he'd grabbed up the paper and headed for his truck.

It was just like the publisher to talk to Ledger. His brother was too nice, too polite. If the publisher had approached *him*, the man would have gotten one hell of a quote. Instead, Ledger had said that the loss of the twins was "killing" his father after twenty-five years of torture.

How could their father still be convinced that Oakley and Jesse Rose were alive? Travers McGraw had this crazy fantasy that the twins had been sold to a couple who, not realizing the babies were stolen, had raised them as their own.

Cull and his brothers had tried to reason with

him. "How could this couple not have heard about the kidnapping? It was in all the newspapers across the country—not to mention on the television news nationally."

His father had no answer, just that he knew the twins were alive and that they would be coming home one day soon.

He knew his father had to believe that. The alternative—that his wife and her alleged lover had kidnapped and killed the twins for money— was too horrible to contemplate.

Under the newspaper fold were the photographs of the babies that his father had provided. Both had the McGraw dark hair, the big blue eyes like their other siblings. Both looked angelic with their bow-shaped mouths and chubby cheeks. They looked like the kind of babies that a person would kill for.

When he'd seen that this year his father was doubling the reward for information, Cull had lost it.

With a curse, he could well imagine what his stepmother was going to say about this. Worse, a reward that size would bring every crank and con man out of the woodwork—just as it had over the years. What had his father been thinking? He was desperate, Cull realized, and the thought scared him.

His father had been sick and didn't seem to

be getting any better. Was this a last-ditch effort to find the twins because he was dying? Cull felt rattled as the idea sunk in. Was their father keeping the truth from them?

Accompanying the story were also photos of Oakley and Jesse Rose digitally age-progressed to show what the twins could look like now. Cull shuddered. How could his father bear to look at these? It was heartbreaking to see what they would have looked like had they lived.

The rest of the story was just a rehash of the kidnapping that summer night twenty-five years ago. What wasn't in the story was that Travers McGraw had sold his most prized quarter horse to raise the ransom demand, and that even after horse trainer Nate Corwin's arrest, the $250,000 ransom had never been recovered.

Nor was there anything about what Travers and Marianne had lost. Not to mention the children left behind. Their mother was in a mental institution and their father had fallen into a debilitating grief and held on to a crazy hope that might be killing him.

Cull wadded up the newspaper and threw it onto the passenger-side floorboard. Had he really thought he could keep this from his family? It was only a matter of time before everyone back at the ranch saw this. His stepmother, Patricia, had long ago tired of this yearly search for the twins. This latest story would set her off royally.

The local weekly paper was only the beginning, he thought with a curse. With the twenty-fifth anniversary of the kidnapping mere days away, other papers would pick up the story and run it, including television news shows.

A part of him wanted to leave town until things died back down again. But as upset as he was with his father, he knew he couldn't run away. His father needed his sons, maybe now more than ever before. Because he might be sicker than they thought. Because once the story was out about the huge reward...

He backed out of his space, wanting to get home and put out as many fires as he could. He'd just thrown the pickup into first gear and gone only a few feet when a young woman stepped off the curb right in front of his truck.

Cull stomped on the brakes, but too late. He heard the truck make contact and saw her fall, disappearing from view before he could leap out, his heart in his throat, to find her sprawled on the pavement.

Chapter Four

Cull knelt beside the dark-haired woman on the pavement, terrified that he might have killed her. He heard people come running out of the café. Someone was calling 9-1-1 as he touched the young woman's shoulder. She didn't stir.

"Is she alive?" someone cried from in front of the café. "The 9-1-1 operator needs to know if she's breathing and how badly she's injured."

Cull took the young woman's slim wrist and felt for a pulse. But his own heart was pounding so hard, he couldn't tell if she had one. He leaned closer to put his cheek against her full lips and prayed.

With a relief that left him weak, he felt her warm breath against his skin. As he drew back, her eyes opened. They were big and a startling blue as bright as the Montana day. A collective sigh of relief moved through the crowd as the woman tried to sit up.

"Don't move," Cull ordered. "An ambulance is on the way."

She shook her head. "An ambulance?" She seemed to see the people around her. "What happened?"

"You stepped out into the street," he said. "I didn't see you until it was too late."

"Please let me up. I'm fine."

"But I hit you with my truck."

She sat up, insistent that she was fine. "Just help me to my feet." She glanced around on the ground next to her. "Where is my purse?"

Just then Sheriff McCall Crawford pushed her way through the crowd. "What happened?" she asked as she knelt beside the woman.

"She stepped into the street," Cull said. "I hit my brakes but—" He'd had so much on his mind. He hadn't even seen her until she'd stepped off the curb.

"I told you," the woman said. "You didn't *hit* me. You might have bumped into me and then… I must have fainted." She looked around her. "If you would just hand me my purse…"

The sheriff glanced around as well, spied her large shoulder bag and handed it to her. "Are you sure you're all right, Miss…?"

"St. James. Nikki St. James."

"Still I'd like the EMTs to have a look at you," the sheriff insisted.

"That really isn't necessary. I feel so silly. If I had been paying attention…"

"No," Cull said. "I was the one not paying attention."

The ambulance arrived and two EMTs jumped out. Cull stepped back to let them get to the woman. Nikki St. James. He frowned. He'd seen that name somewhere recently.

The sheriff pulled him aside. "I'm going to have to write up a report on this. I suggest you call your insurance agent."

"She said she was fine."

"It doesn't appear that you actually *hit* her," the sheriff said. "More than likely she just stepped off the curb and fainted when she realized she'd stepped in front of your truck. But as a precaution, let your insurance office know. They might want you to get her to sign something."

In front of his pickup, the EMTs were helping the woman to her feet. Cull heard her say she needed to go to her rental car. She was late for an appointment.

"I'm not sure you should be driving," one of the EMTs said.

"I can take you wherever you need to go," Cull said, stepping forward. "I agree. You shouldn't drive."

Tears welled in her eyes. "Actually, I would

appreciate that," she said. "I'm not familiar with this area. As shaken as I am, I would probably get lost."

"Where are you headed?"

"A ranch outside of town. The Sundown Stallion Station—are you familiar with it?"

Cull stared at her, feeling all the blood drain from his face. He remembered now where he'd seen her name before. On a scratch pad on his father's desk.

SHERIFF MCCALL CRAWFORD watched Cull help the woman into the passenger side of his pickup. He looked more shaken than Nikki St. James did.

She tried to still the bad feeling that had settled in her stomach as she watched Cull slip behind the wheel. She'd seen his face when the woman had told him where she'd been headed— to his ranch.

McCall could no more help her suspicious nature than she could flap her arms and fly. She'd heard about scams involving people who appeared to have been hit by vehicles. It usually involved a payoff of some kind.

As she watched Cull start his truck and pull away, she couldn't help wondering who Nikki St. James was and, more to the point, what she was after. Did she really have an appointment at the ranch? Or was she a reporter trying to get a foot in the door?

Travers McGraw had been forced to get a locked gate for the ranch entrance because of the publicity about the kidnapping. With the twenty-fifth anniversary coming up next week, McCall worried that Cull had just been scammed.

She looked toward the café, suspecting someone in there had witnessed the accident. Wouldn't hurt to ask and still that tiny voice inside her that told her there was something wrong about this. Also she could use a cup of coffee.

As Cull drove past, she saw him glance at the woman in the passenger seat of his pickup. He looked worried. McCall thought he should be.

Nikki St. James was looking out the side window as they passed. She seemed to be interested in someone inside the café.

McCall turned to see redheaded waitress Abby Pierce standing in the window.

NIKKI TRIED TO RELAX, but she could feel Cull's gaze on her periodically as he drove. That had been more than risky back there. He could very well have killed her.

Her original plan was for Ledger. She'd seen how kindhearted he was. It was one thing to have Travers on her side, but she needed at least one family member she could count on. She'd hoped her stunt would make him more amenable to helping her once he knew who she was.

With Cull, she wasn't sure. At first, he'd been so scared that he would have done anything for her. But then she'd seen his shock when she'd told him where her appointment was.

As he drove south, she said, "Thank you for doing this. I hate to have you going out of your way for me."

"It's not out of my way. Your appointment is with Travers McGraw?"

"Yes."

His gaze was like a laser. "He's my father. I'm Cull McGraw, his oldest son."

She'd feigned surprise. "I knew Whitehorse was a small town, but…"

Nikki saw suspicion in his eyes as they met hers. He would have been a fool not to be suspicious and Cull was no fool. She could see that right away.

She recalled the change in him she'd seen after she'd mentioned her name—and where her appointment was. Had the sheriff said something to him to make him question the accident?

He'd said little since they'd left the small Western town behind them. This part of Montana was rolling prairie where thousands of bison had once ranged. In the distance she could make out the Little Rockies, the only mountains on the horizon.

Wild country, she thought, watching the cowboy out of the corner of her eye. It took a special breed to live in a place where the temperature could change in a heartbeat from fifty above to fifty below zero.

Nikki tried to relax but it was hard. There was an all-male aura about Cull that seemed to fill the pickup cab. She would have had to be in a coma not to be aware of the handsome cowboy, even with his scowling. Did he suspect that what happened back there had been a stunt? She should have stayed with her original plan and waited for Ledger.

Too late to worry about that now. With relief, she saw the sign for the turnoff ahead. Her pulse jumped when she saw the Sundown Stallion Station horse ranch come into view. It reminded her of every horse movie she'd ever seen as a girl. Miles of brilliant green grass fenced in by sparkling white-painted wooden fence that made the place look as if it should be in Kentucky—not the backwoods of Montana.

Cull McGraw hit the remote control on the massive white gate that she knew had been erected not long after the kidnapping to keep out the media and morbidly curious. People not so unlike herself.

The gate swung open without a sound, and after he drove the truck through, it closed behind them.

She was really doing this. Her grandfather had taught her that nothing was out of line to get a story. She would get this one. Her head ached and she was regretting her stunt back in town. It almost got her killed and it hadn't worked. Cull seemed even more distrusting of her.

Out of the corner of her eye, she saw him glance over at her. "How are you feeling?" he asked.

Nervous, scared, excited, terrified. "I have a little headache," she said. She'd hit the pavement harder than she'd planned.

He looked worried and guilty. She felt a sharp stab of her own guilt. But she quickly brushed it away. She had to know the truth about her father. Even as she thought it, a lump formed in her throat.

What if her grandfather was right and she couldn't handle the truth?

This case was definitely more than just a book for her; she could admit that now. She'd come here to prove that Nate Corwin had been innocent.

"Nate Corwin was a philanderer," her grandfather told her the day before she'd left for Whitehorse, Montana. "Of course, he was having an affair with Marianne McGraw. He loved women with money. It's why he married your mother."

"I don't believe that."

"Too bad you can't ask your mother, but she's off on some shopping spree in Paris, I hear. But then again, she'd just defend him like she always did," Wendell St. James had said. "Don't come crying to me when you find out the worst."

"I've never come crying to you," she'd pointed out.

"Smart girl," he'd said.

When she'd first confronted her mother about what she'd found out, Georgia had told her that her father had never liked Nate.

"It was because Nate was his own man," her mother had told her. "Daddy tried to hire him right after we got married. But your father flat out refused. 'I'm a horse trainer, not some flunky who sits behind a desk, especially a newspaper one.'" She'd chuckled. "You can imagine how that went over."

Nikki could. "So there is no truth in the newspaper accounts that he was cheating on you?"

Her mother had smiled. "Your father loved me and adored you. He couldn't wait to finish his work at the ranch and get back to us."

"Why would he leave us if that were true?" she'd asked.

"Because his true love was his work and horses. Yes, he was away a lot because of his job, but he wouldn't have cheated," her mother had said simply.

Cheated? Or done much worse?

"I'll get you some aspirin when we reach the house," Cull said now as he drove along the tree-lined drive. "If you feel too ill, I'm sure you could get your appointment changed to another day."

She shook her head. "Aspirin would be greatly appreciated. I really can't put this off."

The sun flickered through the dark green of the leaves. Ahead, the big white two-story house loomed.

Nikki looked over at him, torn between apprehension and excitement. She was finally going to get into the McGraw house. "I'm a little anxious about my appointment."

"Yes, your appointment."

She didn't like the way he said it and decided to hit him with the worst of it and get it over with. "I'm nervous about meeting your father. I'd thought maybe he would have told you. I'm a true crime writer. I'm going to write a book on the kidnapping."

Cull swore as he brought the pickup to a dust-boiling stop in front of the house. He seemed at a loss for words as he stared at her and she stared right back as if unable to understand the problem. A muscle jumped in his jaw, his hands gripping the steering wheel so tightly she thought it might snap. Those blue eyes had turned to ice and peered out just as cold and hard.

Fortunately, they were both saved. The front door of the house opened; a woman appeared. Nikki knew at once that she was the notorious Patricia "Patty" Owens McGraw.

She'd been able to learn little about Patricia Owens, the nanny, or Patty Owens McGraw, the second Mrs. McGraw, other than the fact that she was from a neighboring town and had gotten Ted to divorce Marianne so he could marry her sixteen years ago.

The only photo she'd seen of Patty the nanny had been a blurry black and white that had run in the newspaper at the time of the kidnapping. It showed a teenager with straight brown hair, thick glasses and a timid look in her pale eyes.

That's why Nikki was surprised to see the woman who came out to the edge of the porch. Patty was now winter-wheat blonde, sans the ugly eyeglasses, and any sign of timidity was long gone. She wore a large rock on her ring finger and several nice-sized diamonds on each earlobe—all catching the sunlight and glittering wildly. The dress she wore looked straight from some swank New York City boutique, as did her high heels and the rest of her tasteful adornments.

Patty had been nineteen the summer when she'd gone to work as a nanny at the ranch, which would make her about forty-four now. Her husband, Travers McGraw, was sixty.

Frowning, Patricia spun on one high heel and marched back into the house, leaving the front door standing open. She didn't look happy to see that Cull had a woman with him. Had Travers told his wife about Nikki?

She stared at the rambling, infamous house she'd only seen in grainy newspaper photographs—and always from a distance. Was she really going to pull this off? Her heart was a low thunder in her chest as she opened her door and stepped out of the pickup.

She tried to wrangle in her fears. The clock was ticking. She'd done this all before. Once she showed up, anyone with a secret started getting nervous. It usually didn't take long before the mystery began to unravel.

Nikki had only days to discover the truth before the anniversary, which was usually plenty of time to make progress on a book. But from the look on Patricia's face before she'd disappeared back inside the house, and Cull's cursing inside his pickup, it was going to be an uphill battle.

CULL KNEW HE'D acted impulsively. He should have listened to Sheriff Crawford. Instead he'd offered the woman a ride only to realize she was going to the same place he was—and for a reason he would never have imagined.

"True crime writer?" he repeated as he climbed out of the pickup after her. Had his father lost his mind?

He'd looked up to see his stepmother appear in the open doorway looking like she'd sucked on a lemon before she'd gone back inside in a snit. Did she already know about this? If not, when she found out, she would go ballistic. He felt the same way himself.

Cull wanted to storm into the house and demand to know what the hell his father had been thinking. Not that it would do any good, he thought, remembering the newspaper story.

He saw Nikki St. James rub her temple where she'd hit the pavement. Even if she'd stepped in front of his pickup on purpose, he grimaced at the thought that he could have killed her. He reminded himself that he'd promised her aspirin, while a part of him wished he'd almost hit the gas harder back in town.

Mostly, he was just anxious to see his father. The only one more anxious, he noticed, was Nikki St. James. His father had no idea what he'd done.

Raised voices came from the house. Had Patricia seen the newspaper article and the increased reward her husband was offering? If so, she was already on the warpath. Even after twenty-five years, there was too much curiosity about their family. So much so that they seldom had guests out to the house. They'd isolated themselves from the world and now his father had invited the worst kind of reporter into their home.

What did his father even know about this Nikki St. James? Had he checked out her credentials? One thing was obvious, Cull thought as he walked with her toward the house. All Hades was about to be unleashed.

He hesitated at the porch steps, noticing something he hadn't before. Clearly this woman wasn't from around here, given the way she was dressed—in slacks, a white blouse, pale coral tank and high heels—and the faint accent he hadn't been able to place. It definitely wasn't Montanan.

"Hold up," Cull said to her backside as she continued up the steps.

She stopped midway but didn't turn until he joined her. She looked pale and for a moment he worried that she was more hurt that she'd let on. She touched her temple. He could see that it was red, a bruise forming, and his heart ached at the sight. No matter who she was or what she was doing here, he hadn't meant to hurt her. If only he'd been paying attention…

"Maybe you should sit down for a minute," he suggested.

"I'm fine. Really."

She didn't look fine and he felt guilty in spite of how he felt about her being here. He actually felt sorry for her. She had no idea what she was getting into.

"Look, I'm not sure whose idea this was, but it was a bad one. What you're about to walk into… My family—"

He didn't get the chance to warn her further, let alone try to talk her out of this before it was too late. His stepsister, Kitten, stormed out of the house and across the wide porch to block their path. Kitten was sixteen and at the age that she thought everything was about her. He could see from the scowl on her face that she'd been arguing with her mother—as usual.

"My mother is impossible," the teen said around a wad of gum. She was dressed in a crop top and a very short skirt and strappy sandals, as if headed for town, a big expensive leather purse slung over one shoulder. "Can I borrow your truck?"

"No, Kitten," he said, and started to push past her.

"One of these days you'll regret being so mean to me," the girl said, then seemed to see Nikki. "Who's this?" she demanded, narrowing her eyes suspiciously as she took in the woman next to him. "You finally get a girlfriend, Cull?"

Chapter Five

Nikki guessed this teenager blocking their way must be Patty's child, the one she'd brought back with her to the ranch when the girl was just a baby. That would have been about sixteen years ago, making the young woman standing in front of her sixteen, if Nikki's math was correct.

The nanny, Patricia "Patty" Owens, had left the ranch after the kidnapping only to return nine years later with a baby. The father of the child had never been revealed. Was it possible this teen was Travers's?

"Back off, Kitten," Cull said as he and Nikki ascended the rest of the steps. "I'm not in the mood."

"Why is everyone in such a bad mood today?" the teen demanded, clearly taking it personally.

Nikki stepped through the front door, followed by Cull, then stopped, wanting to take it all in. But she wasn't given a chance.

"Cull? Is that Ms. St. James with you?" a deep male voice called from an open doorway off to her right. "Please have her come in."

"I'll get you those aspirin," Cull said as Nikki turned toward the open doorway.

Travers McGraw seemed preoccupied, one hand on his forehead, his elbow resting on the large oak desk in front of him.

Nikki stopped in the open doorway, studying him for a moment. She'd seen dozens of photographs of Travers McGraw, most taken right after the kidnapping. He'd been a big, strong, handsome man, dark-haired with the same pale blue eyes as the two sons she'd seen.

The past twenty-five years had not been kind to him. While his hair hadn't turned as white as his ex-wife Marianne's, it was shot with gray and there were deep lines etched around his eyes. He seemed to have shrunk in size, his body thin, his shoulders stooped.

But as he looked up, his smile was welcoming.

"Mr. McGraw, I'm Nikki St. James," she said, stepping forward to extend her hand. "The crime writer."

He seemed to come alive as he got to his feet. Hope burned bright in his eyes with such intensity that the weight of it hit her hard. He was depending on her to solve the case.

"Please, call me Travers," he said as he shook her hand, clasping it with both of his. "I'm so glad you're here. I didn't hear you come in." He glanced toward the open doorway. "I thought you were going to call for directions to the ranch."

"Actually, I ran into your son Cull in town—" literally, she thought "—and he brought me out."

"Wonderful," Travers said a little distractedly. "All that matters is that you're here and you're going to find out what happened to the twins." He rubbed his temples as if he had a headache, too.

She hoped she didn't make it worse. She started to reiterate that she couldn't make any promises, but she didn't get the words out before Patty burst into the room.

"Tell me I'm misinformed," Patricia said, looking from Nikki to her husband, her blue eyes wild with anger. "Tell me you haven't brought this…this…woman into our home."

"Patricia." He sighed, looking defeated again. "This is not the place to—"

"*Not the place?* This has to stop. I thought we decided—"

"*You* decided," he said, looking a little less beat down. "I will never stop looking for them."

His words fanned the flames of the woman's

fury, but seemed to leave her speechless for a moment.

"We need to talk," Patricia said to her husband between gritted teeth.

"I'm sure we will," he agreed as he sat back down behind his desk and motioned for Nikki to take a seat. "But right now I need you to leave and close the door behind you."

All color drained from the woman's face. Clearly appalled, she stormed out, slamming the door behind her.

"I apologize for my wife's behavior," he said after a moment. "I hope this doesn't change your mind."

Nikki shook her head. "Not at all." It wasn't the first time she'd run into a relative who didn't want anyone digging into the past. It wouldn't be the last.

She hadn't expected to get much out of Patty Owens McGraw anyway. But if the answers were on this ranch, she told herself she would find them even without the woman's help.

"You said that I would be allowed the run of the ranch," Nikki reminded him. "I hope you haven't changed your mind."

He shook his head. "If there is even the slightest chance that you might find out the truth… Just let me know what you need from me. I should warn you. My wife isn't the only one who might be opposed to this."

"Your sons."

He nodded. "Also my lawyer and a close family friend who was in the house that night. They both are quite adamant that this is a mistake. I completely disagree with them, understand. But you might find getting information from them difficult, and I'm sorry about that."

"I've worked with families before that were... skeptical," she said.

He smiled at her understatement of the current situation and raked a hand through his graying hair, looking apologetic. "I had hoped that once you were here it might be easier. Please don't think I'm a coward for not telling my sons. They don't want me to be disappointed again and I really wasn't up to arguing before you got here. With so much time having passed and no new evidence..."

"I hate to get your hopes up as well, but I can promise you that I will do everything I can to find out the truth. I'd like to take a look around the house and the ranch," Nikki said, getting to her feet. "But first if someone can show me to my room. I'm afraid my car and luggage are still in town."

"Not a problem. I'll have someone pick it up for you," he said as he rose from behind his desk.

There was a tap at the door before it swung in. She turned to see Cull silhouetted in the doorway. He stepped forward, holding out a glass of water and two aspirin. She took them as she listened to Travers asking his son to see that Nikki's car was brought out to the ranch.

"But first if you wouldn't mind showing her to the guest room," the older man finished.

"I'll show her to her room," came a voice from the open doorway. It was the teenager who'd accosted her earlier on the porch steps. It was clear that Kitten had been close by, eavesdropping.

The insincere smile had an almost demented quality to it. Nikki wondered again about Patricia's daughter, the mystery child she'd brought back to the ranch years ago.

"Kitten, this is Nikki St. James," Travers said, introducing them. "She will be staying with us while she works on a book about the kidnapping."

The girl raised one brow. "Fascinating." She sounded like her mother, the word just snide enough.

"I want you to be nice to her," he said.

"Of course, Daddy," Kitten said, almost purring. "Later, can I borrow your car to go into town? I'm meeting some friends."

"You just got your license. I'm not sure that's a good idea. What did your mother say?"

"She said she didn't care if I went after dinner, but…" She mugged a face. "She's afraid I'm going to wreck her precious car."

"You can take mine," he said, sounding tired. "Just promise me that you'll be careful and come home whatever time your mother tells you."

The teen rushed to him and kissed his cheek. "Thank you, Daddy." As she turned, she mugged a face at Nikki.

Travers turned to Nikki. "Leave me your keys. Cull will see that everything is taken care of."

She thanked him as she handed them over, only to find Cull standing behind her. He scooped the keys up from the desk and pocketed them, then left without a word. She figured he'd been too surprised earlier to voice his displeasure, but his swearing had given her a clue as to how he felt about her being here.

"We can talk after dinner, Ms. St. James," Travers said as she and Kitten started out of the room.

"Nikki, please," she said, stopping in the doorway.

He smiled. "I can't tell you how glad I am that you're here, Nikki. Dinner is at six. It's informal."

She nodded and followed Kitten out the door.

"Can you point out the wing where the twins' nursery was?" Nikki asked the girl.

Kitten smiled. "Of course."

They'd barely left the room before Patricia, who'd clearly been waiting only yards away, rushed into her husband's office, slamming the door behind her. Nikki could hear her raised voice as Kitten led her up the wide stairway.

CULL COULD HAVE handed off the job of retrieving Nikki St. James's car and luggage from town to a couple of the hired hands. After all, he was as unhappy about this turn of events as his stepmother. He was also anxious to talk to his father.

But right now Patricia was chewing Travers's ear, and the best place to be was far from the house until some of the dust settled.

Also, he wanted to know more about Nikki St. James before he confronted his father.

"I could use your help," he said when he found his younger brother in the barn. "Can you drive me into town?"

"Can't Boone do it?" Ledger asked as he rubbed a hand down the long neck of the newest horse.

"He's gone to pick up that stallion Dad bought last week."

Ledger sighed. "Fine. What's going on in the

house, or do I even have to guess?" he asked as they walked along the path next to the house.

Even from here, Cull could hear Patricia's voice raised in fury. He and his brother usually escaped to the horse barns when their father and Patricia were arguing. That's how he'd known where he would find Ledger, especially today after the newspaper article.

"We have a surprise guest."

Ledger blinked. *"Guest?"* He perked up so much that Cull realized for some unknown reason his brother had hoped it was Abby Pierce, the waitress at the Whitehorse Café and his brother's former love. For some reason, Ledger thought that Abby was going to come back to him.

"Dad has hired a crime writer to do a book on the kidnapping," he said before Ledger's unrealistic hopes could be raised further.

"What?"

"I'll tell you all about it on the way into town."

True to his word, he told his brother everything he knew, which wasn't that much.

"Dad has lost his mind," Ledger said when he'd finished.

"Seems that way. She's going to be staying at the house. That's why I need to pick up her car for her. According to what it says on the key, it's a blue compact with Billings plates. We should find it parked near the café where I found you this morning."

"Wait, how did she get to the ranch?"

"I drove her. It's a long story. But suffice it to say, we're apparently stuck with her for a while," Cull said.

"So what does she look like?" his brother asked, turning toward him as they reached town.

He hesitated a little too long.

Ledger laughed. "I've never seen you at a loss for words when it comes to describing a woman."

"It's not like that with this one. She's all right to look at, but I don't trust her."

"Well, once she realizes there is nothing new to write about, she'll leave."

"Let's hope so. I'm just worried about how much damage she'll do before that. Dad—"

"He looks bad, doesn't he?"

Cull nodded around the sudden lump in his throat as he pulled up behind the rental car parked on the main drag of Whitehorse. "I'm going to do what I have to to protect him. Starting by finding out everything I can about Nikki St. James."

NIKKI AND KITTEN were almost to the top of the stairs when Kitten turned abruptly. Swinging around, her large purse hit Nikki, throwing her off balance. Her gaze shot up to Kitten's.

The teen looked surprised for a moment, then a small smile curled her lips as Nikki teetered on her high heels. She grabbed wildly for the handrail. The tips of her fingers glossed over it, but she couldn't find purchase. She could feel herself going over backward.

At the last minute, Kitten grabbed her hand, the two of them almost tumbling down the stairs as Nikki fought to get her feet back under her.

"That was a close call," the teen said in a mocking tone. "You really should be more careful. People in town say this house is cursed. Terrible things have happened here." She blinked wide blue eyes. "We should get you to your room. You don't look well."

With that she turned and started up the stairs. It was all Nikki could do not to grab the back of her shirt and fling her down the stairs. She was shaking from the near fall and still a little unsteady on her feet. It didn't help that the two aspirin Cull had given her hadn't started to work yet on her headache.

Nikki had faced opposition before. She'd also put herself in dangerous situations. It went with the territory. But as she stared after Kitten, she realized that she'd glimpsed something in the teen that frightened her more than the near accident.

She would have to watch her back in this house—just as her grandfather had warned her. Except it wasn't the kidnapper she apparently had to worry about. But it could be the spawn of one of the kidnappers, she thought, reminded of the look in Kitten's eyes moments ago.

While Nikki thought the purse incident had been an accident, the girl hadn't been that sorry it had happened.

Chapter Six

When McCall wanted information about White-horse, she went to her grandmother. Even though Pepper lived on Winchester Ranch miles from town, she had always known what was going on in the county sooner than most.

McCall hadn't doubted that she would remember the McGraw kidnapping.

"Remember it?" Pepper exclaimed after the two of them were seated in the living room. For most of her life, McCall had never laid eyes on Winchester Ranch—or her grandmother. Pepper had denied that McCall was her grand-daughter until events had thrown them together. Now they had a mutual respect for each other that verged on love.

"I dug this out after you called," Pepper said, and handed her a file stuffed with newspaper and magazine articles.

"All this is about the kidnapping?"

Her grandmother nodded.

McCall glanced at a couple of articles, but this wasn't what she was looking for. She turned to her grandmother. "I need the dirt. The rumors. The things your old cook used to bring you."

Pepper laughed. "I'd almost forgotten about her." The woman had drugged her grandmother to keep her from demanding too much. McCall had never understood the relationship between the two women, since her grandmother knew what was going on and did nothing about it. Apparently Pepper had some affection for the woman to put up with it for so long.

"There were lots of rumors, if that's what you want. Marianne McGraw and the horse trainer, Nate Corwin. Travers McGraw and the nanny, Patricia Owens. Then there were disgruntled ranch hands looking to make a buck. There is the former ranch manager and close friend Blake Ryan. But I always suspected the lawyer. He was one sleazy bastard, that one."

"Jim Waters? But he's still the McGraw lawyer."

Pepper raised a brow. "That should tell you something."

"That he's trusted?"

"That Travers lives in a houseful of vipers and doesn't realize it," her grandmother said.

"The man married Patricia Owens." She raised a brow as if that said everything.

"I suppose you heard—"

"About the true crime writer?" Pepper laughed at her granddaughter's surprise. "Also heard that Patty threw a fit."

"Nikki St. James is writing a book about the kidnapping," McCall said.

Her grandmother lifted another finely tuned eyebrow. "You don't trust her?"

"Something happened in town—"

"That little *accident* in front of the White-horse Café?"

McCall laughed. "You must have thought the same thing I did."

"The young woman staged it."

She nodded. "I'm just not sure what she thought it would get her. Cull McGraw was driving the pickup. He's the oldest. He was upset and gave her a ride out to the ranch. But when he found out who she was, I'm sure he was suspicious."

"Probably," Pepper agreed. "Those McGraw sons are smart as well as good-looking."

"I've heard there is no love lost between them and Patricia."

"What do you expect? No one in town can stand her," Pepper said. "The question you should be asking yourself is why Travers married her to begin with."

"He's a nice guy. She was young, had a baby, needed his help," the sheriff suggested.

"Or she had something on him," her grandmother suggested. "Guilt is a huge motivator—if not blackmail."

NIKKI PAUSED AT the top of the stairs for a moment to look back at the house. She felt she needed to catch her breath—and not just from her near fall. She still couldn't believe she was in this house—her father had once walked some of these halls. From what she'd gathered in her research, Nate Corwin had been a frequent guest.

But she wondered if it had been at Travers's request—or his wife's.

Pushing that thought away, she turned to look back down the stairs.

She'd wanted to see the inside of this house from the moment she'd found the newspaper clippings and discovered how her father had really died.

Now she looked around at all the grandeur, not surprised how beautiful it was. She'd read that Travers McGraw had built the house for his first wife as an anniversary gift. The two had started out relatively poor, living in a small house some distance away. But when he'd begun siring prize-winning quarter horses, he'd had the house built for Marianne. By that time, she had already given him three sons—Cull, Boone and Ledger.

He'd spared no expense on the house and it had no doubt become the talk of the town as well as the county. Was that what had given the kidnapper the idea of taking her two youngest children?

After meeting him, Nikki had hated to get Travers McGraw's hopes up. He seemed a fragile man who'd been through too much. She wondered if another disappointment might kill him.

But she had hoped that there was something here to find—someone who had something to hide. She thought of Patricia. The former nanny had ended up with Travers, and if she played her cards right, she could end up with the ranch, since he didn't seem long for this world.

Except for the fact that Travers still had three grown sons. Did she plan to get rid of them, too? So why would she have kidnapped the twins all those years ago? What would have been her motive?

True, she'd implicated Marianne McGraw. But even if she wanted to be rid of both the wife and the babies, it seemed a little too desperate as a means to an end. Especially if that end was getting Travers McGraw.

Kidnappings usually were about money. But as far as Nikki knew, the ransom money had never been spent. Because the kidnappers had accidentally killed the twins and had gotten too scared? She thought of the broken rung halfway down the ladder. Had the kidnapper fallen? Had he dropped one of the babies or both of them?

For all the research she'd done, Nikki had too many questions still. All her instincts, though, told her that the answers were here in this house. Someone in this house knew at least a piece of the truth. Once she had all those pieces...

"Are you coming?" Kitten demanded from down the hall.

Nikki sighed and turned to follow the teen. She couldn't help looking into each room they passed, feeling a tingle of excitement. The house was beautifully decorated. Had that been Marianne's doing? Or the new Mrs. McGraw?

Kitten had stopped at the end of the hall. Nikki knew the layout of the house. Downstairs was the large living room, Travers's office, the master bedroom and a huge farm kitchen and dining room.

Upstairs at the back part of the house were the bedrooms for the children and nanny. They were arranged down a long hallway that ran north to south, with the nanny's larger room and the playroom at the south end.

When Nikki joined Kitten, she turned north down a short hallway. Nikki recalled that the twins' nursery had been on the south wing—next to Patricia's. She glanced in that direction. The hallway was dark. A heavy silence seemed to hunker in its shadowy depths.

"This way," Kitten said, and walked to the end of the hall, where she opened a door into a room decorated in shades of blue. "This was Cull's room growing up." She smiled at Nikki's surprise.

She shot Kitten a look. "This is the room I'm staying in?" She'd distinctly heard Travers tell her the guest room.

The teen gave her an innocent smile. "You want to be in this wing, right? Otherwise, they're going to stick you away somewhere since no one stays on these wings anymore."

Nikki looked out the window and saw the addition to the house that had been added after the kidnapping so Travers would be closer to his remaining children. Past it, she saw what appeared to be a pool and pool house.

While what the girl said made sense, Nikki knew what Kitten was up to. The one person who would be most upset about her staying in his room would be Cull. But she decided she would play along and deal with Cull when the time came.

"It's a lovely room." She glanced around, chilled a little at the thought that he hadn't stayed in this room since the kidnapping. This entire wing had been left exactly as it had been. What had he heard that night? Or was it true that he, like the others, had slept right through the kidnapping?

She realized she was rubbing her bare arms as if to warm them. It wasn't cold in the room. On the contrary, the air felt heavy. It was being in Cull's childhood room, being in this house, being this close to the room where the twins had been taken from, she told herself.

"Creepy, huh," Kitten said, no doubt seeing her reaction. Kitten didn't miss much.

"Yes," Nikki agreed. Something horrible had happened in this house. A kidnapping that had probably led to the murder of two innocent babies. And Nate Corwin had been in this house. Possibly climbed the same stairs she had, maybe even walked down this very hallway. What if her grandfather was right? What if she found out that her father had been part of the kidnapping? Part of something even worse?

She thought of Marianne McGraw's snow-white hair and blank, empty eyes, and shuddered inwardly.

Kitten moved to the window and pulled back the drapes, blinding her for a moment. Past the teen, Nikki could see the barn and corrals where her father had worked. Beyond them was the bunkhouse where he'd lived. She'd seen the layout of the ranch from an aerial photo that had been shot after the kidnapping. Since then, some cabins had been added at the back of the property. Was that where Travers's sons lived?

Turning, she watched Kitten pick up a toy cowboy on a plastic horse from a shelf near the bed. "No one comes up here but Tilly to clean. So," she said as she put the horse back on the shelf and met Nikki's gaze, "you'll have it all to yourself. Good luck. Tilly swears she's seen ghosts up here and heard babies crying."

Kitten was trying to scare her *again*, not realizing that what scared her most would be the truth about that night.

"Thank you for showing me to the room, Kitten."

"It's Katherine. Only my family calls me Kitten."

"Duly noted." Her head throbbed. She couldn't wait for this young woman to leave. "I might lie down for a while before dinner."

"Yes, dinner," Kitten said, and smiled. "All the family and my father's attorney will be there. I can't wait for everyone to meet you."

As HE RETURNED from town with Nikki's rental car, Cull heard Kitten's and her mother's raised voices. He quickly stepped into the office, hoping to find his father and avoid the latest upset.

The room was empty. A small fire burned in the fireplace and the latest edition of the *Milk River Courier* was spread on his father's desk. He stepped closer. One glance at the headline about the kidnapping and he let out a curse. Getting rid of the other newspaper before the cook brought it into the house hadn't done any good. Wadding up this newspaper, he angrily tossed it into the fire as his father came into the room.

Travers spotted the burning newspaper and gave Cull a sympathetic shake of his head. "I appreciate you trying to spare me, but I've already read it." He joined him in front of the fire and laid a hand on his shoulder. "Even if I hadn't, you can't burn every newspaper in town."

"I hate for you to have to go through this again," Cull said.

His father smiled wearily. "*I* was the one who contacted the newspaper, son. Anyway, it isn't something I can ever forget."

"We should talk about this woman—"

"Nikki St. James. Thank you for bringing her out to the ranch. You and Ledger, I understand, went in and brought back her car. Please see that her luggage is taken upstairs."

"I intend to take it up myself," Cull said. "But I have to ask you. Are you sure about this?" He'd gotten on his phone after Ledger had dropped him off and done some research on the woman. He'd hoped to find something that would dissuade his father from going through with this.

Unfortunately, what he found was a professional website, heartwarming reviews and a pretty astounding track record for unearthing new information on true crimes. He could see how his father might have been impressed that she wanted to do a book on the kidnapping.

Travers McGraw didn't answer right away. He lowered himself into his chair before meeting Cull's gaze. "It's been twenty-five years. Your stepmother is right about one thing—I can't keep doing this to myself or to all of you. This is it, Cull. If nothing comes of this book, then I'm done."

Cull let out a sigh of relief. "I know how much this means to you, but I'm glad to hear you feel that way. I'm worried it's going to kill you otherwise."

His father nodded. "So please, help this woman with anything she needs and ask your brothers to do the same. I'll appeal to Patty and Kitten, though I don't hold out much hope for their cooperation." His smile was sad. "I can't help but hope."

Cull wanted to change his father's mind, to argue that he didn't know anything about this woman and that bringing her into the house could lead to disastrous consequences.

He put a hand on his father's shoulder and quickly swallowed back the words, surprised how thin the shoulder felt, how weak his father looked. "I best get her luggage to her."

As he left his father's office, his stepmother came flying in, slamming the door behind her. Cull picked up Nikki St. James's designer suitcase and, taking the stairs three at a time, was at the top when he heard his stepsister call to him from the ground floor below.

"I put her in your old room," Kitten said. He stopped, nearly losing his balance as he turned to look back at her. She stood smiling that impish smile at him.

"Why would you put her in my old room?" he demanded through gritted teeth.

"Because that's the one that Tilly says is haunted the worst." She laughed and took off out the front door.

He almost forgot himself. That girl had needed a good tanning for years. Although he doubted it would do any good. She was just like her mother, spoiled and impossible, he thought as he heard the raised voices coming from the office. Maybe it wasn't his father's loss that was killing him. Maybe it was Patricia and her... daughter.

He often wondered why his father put up with the two of them. Travers had raised Kitten as his own. According to the scuttlebutt in town, she *was* his own. The story was that they'd been lovers all along and that—on top of the kidnapping of her babies—their affair pushed Marianne McGraw over the edge.

For the story to be true, then Patty and his father had renewed their relationship in secret. He and Ledger would have been in high school when Kitten was conceived.

Cull shook his head as he topped the stairs. He didn't have time to speculate on the past. Right now, he was headed for his childhood bedroom in the wing of the house that he hadn't entered in years.

After the kidnapping, he and his brother had been moved to other rooms, closer to his parents. That was back before they took his mother away one day, never to return.

As he walked down the hallway, he couldn't help being furious with Nikki St. James for bringing up bad memories already—and she hadn't even begun writing the darned book.

Who knew what she might discover?

That thought turned his blood to slush. He'd buried so many memories of that night and the days after. And now she would be poking around, forcing him to relive them. Worse, reminding him of the secret he'd sworn he'd keep until his dying day.

NIKKI FRESHENED UP, waiting to make sure that Kitten had left. Cull's childhood bedroom was all boy, from the blue decor to the many male toys. He'd just turned seven at the time of the kidnapping, so he must not have spent much time in this beautifully decorated room before this wing was abandoned. Which explained why the room looked as if a little boy might return at any moment.

Hoping the coast was clear, she went to the door, opened it and peered out into the hallway. It was empty. Hearing nothing, she stepped out, easing the door closed behind her, and started down the hall. All of the doors to the rooms were closed.

Where the other hallway she and Kitten had come down intersected, she stopped and peered around the corner. Seeing no one, she headed for the south wing of the sprawling house. This was where the nursery was located, along with a playroom and nanny quarters. This was where Patty Owens had lived before the kidnapping.

The twins' bedroom room was at the end of the hallway across from the nanny's room next to a back stairway.

As Nikki neared the end of the hall, she slowed and glanced over her shoulder. That same uneasy feeling she'd felt earlier in Cull's former room now washed over her. While immaculately clean and cared for, the wing still had an abandoned feel. No wonder the housekeeper, Tilly, thought she felt ghosts up here. That is, if Kitten hadn't just been trying to scare Nikki with the story.

Though it wasn't necessary, she found herself tiptoeing the rest of the way. The door to the twins' room was closed. She took hold of the doorknob and jerked her hand back as if she'd been burned. It wasn't until she touched it again that she realized it wasn't hot—it was ice-cold. The heat must be turned off in this wing.

She turned the knob.

Chapter Seven

As the door swung into the former nursery, Nikki was hit with a draft of freezing cold air. Movement. Her heart slammed against her ribs. It took a moment for her eyes to adjust to the dim light. A curtain billowed in the wind. It snapped, then fell silent for a moment before another gust raised it like a ghost coming through the window.

She let her heart rate drop back to normal before she stepped into the room. The wall by the window was painted in alternating blue-and-pink stripes. Someone had started a pastoral mural on the wall opposite the cribs. It had faded. This room, like Cull's, gave her a feeling of being transported back to another more innocent time.

Two cribs were positioned side by side on the opposite wall. She could see the horse patterns on the matching mattress sets. One with a blue background, the other pink. Nikki moved closer, stopping when she saw the tiny covers pulled back. Was that how the kidnapper had left them?

She thought she caught the scent of baby powder, a sick sweetness that turned her stomach. She fought her revulsion and moved to the window, careful not to touch anything. The room still felt like a crime scene.

At the window, she saw the faint dark residue where fingerprints had been lifted off the windowsill and frame. Nikki wondered if the window had been left open by the housekeeper or if the kidnapper had left it like this.

The breeze stirred the cute pink-and-blue curtains and the white sheers under them. On closer inspection she saw that the fabric had faded pink-and-blue prints of tiny ducks. Something about that brought a lump to her throat.

As often as she'd thought of the twins since she'd found the newspaper clippings and discovered her father's involvement with the McGraws, this was the first time she'd felt the full weight of what had happened here.

The cold draft of air seemed to move through the room. She shivered as it curled around her neck. She couldn't imagine anything worse than losing a child—let alone two.

She rubbed her bare arms to chase away the

chill as she considered the nursery. Whoever had prepared this room for the twins must have been excited for their arrival.

Had it been their mother, Marianne? Or had they paid someone to get it ready? Nanny Patty Owens had been here several weeks before the twins were born. Nikki couldn't imagine the woman she'd met downstairs taking such pains to prepare for another woman's infants. But maybe Patty had been as unthreatening as she'd appeared back then.

Nikki moved closer so she could look out the window to the ground below. The FBI had found boot prints in the soft earth where a ladder had been placed against the side of the house—just like in the Lindbergh case.

"What are you doing in here?"

Nikki jumped, startled by the low husky male voice directly behind her. She hadn't heard anyone come down the hall, let alone enter the room. She suspected the tall, broad-shouldered, slim-hipped cowboy now standing only inches away had planned it that way as she met Cull's blue-eyed glare with one of her own.

"Your father gave me the run of the house, including this room," she said defiantly. He'd scared her and she could tell he was glad of it. She'd scared him earlier. Did he think that made them even?

He looked toward the open window. "There's nothing here to find."

"Thank you, but I'll be the judge of that."

His hair was long and dark, in stark contrast to the pale blue of his eyes. The resemblance between the McGraw men made her think of Kitten, with her long dark hair and intense blue eyes. She could have been a McGraw.

"Is the window always left open like that?" she asked, looking past him. She could see part of the horse barn where her father had worked as the window parted the curtains.

"Tilly closes it, but when my father comes up, especially this time of year, he opens it so it's as it was that night when the twins were found missing." His gaze, which had been on the window for a moment, moved to hers. There was a primal maleness to Cull that resonated in those eyes. It was as if he could see his effect on her. That, too, seemed to please him.

"You really have no idea what you've gotten yourself into," he said with a shake of his head.

"I've done other books that involved murders and—"

His laugh cut her off. "You feel it, don't you?" She started to ask what he was talking about, but he didn't give her a chance. "This house, this…" He waved his arms, his gaze boring into hers. "Evil that an open window will never blow from this house."

"If you're going to tell me about the ghosts—"

"That Tilly has seen?" He smiled as he shook his head. "No, I'm talking about a place where something horrible has happened. The evil stays. Like a residue. Like a bad feeling. Like part of the furnishings. You can never get rid of it."

"So why do *you* stay here?"

"Because raising horses is in my blood. But I don't live in the house. I have a cabin on the ranch. You couldn't get me to spend a night on this wing or even under this roof. You don't believe in ghosts? You will."

She thought of how Travers McGraw looked ghostlike. He didn't appear to have fared much better than his former wife. He was thin to the point of gaunt, his face ashen, making her fear he hadn't been well. More than ever, she thought that was why he'd allowed her the opportunity to write the book on the kidnapping.

"What is wrong with your father?"

The abrupt change of subject caught Cull off guard for a moment. "What do you think? All this has taken a toll on him."

"Has he seen a doctor?"

"You seriously can't see what has caused his decline?"

"It has to be more than the kidnapping. He really doesn't look well."

Cull sighed. "I've been trying to get him to see a doctor. He's stubborn."

"Like his son."

He shot her a warning look. "Let's say you are as good as your book publicist claims. What you uncover about the case could kill him."

"Is that what you're afraid of? Or is there a reason you don't want the truth to come out? Maybe some secret of your own?"

Something flickered in those deep blue eyes, but he quickly hid it. "I had just turned seven years old."

"Plenty old enough to remember that night. Maybe remember more than you've ever told anyone."

She thought she saw him flinch as if she'd hit too close to the truth. "I've found that often family members know more than they want to tell. They're covering for someone or they're worried what will happen if they tell."

Cull shook his head. "I'm just worried about my family and what you're about to do to it."

"You could help me."

He shook his head. "Have you not heard a word I've said?"

"Your father needs to know what happened that night. Can't you see that?"

Cull let out a low curse. "He already knows what happened."

"No, I don't think so. I don't believe your mother had anything to do with the kidnapping. Nor do I believe Nate Corwin did."

He looked surprised. "Then who?"

She cocked a brow at him. "That's what I'm going to find out. With your help."

"Sorry, but there isn't anything to find. You're wasting your time. Worse, you're giving my father false hope."

"What if hope is the only thing keeping him alive?"

"I almost feel sorry for you," Cull said. "You start digging in the past and all you're going to do is stir up more trouble than even you can handle."

"That almost sounds like a threat."

He shrugged. "Just remember. I tried to warn you." He turned toward the door. Over his shoulder he said, "Dinner's ready."

"I'm going to find out the truth with or without your help," she called to his retreating backside.

He stopped in the doorway to look back at her. "Let me know when you have it solved because I've spent years trying to figure out what happened that night and I was actually in the house. I heard Patty's screams. I still hear them."

NIKKI STARED AT HIM. The man threw her off balance. She would have to be very careful around him, she thought just an instant before the sound of high heels could be heard making a noisy, angry tattoo in the hallway as they approached.

They both looked toward the doorway as Patty McGraw appeared. Nikki heard Cull curse under his breath.

"What are the two of you doing in here?" Patricia demanded. She looked from her stepson to Nikki and back. "You brought her in here, Cull? What is wrong with you and the rest of this family?"

"She found her way on her own," he said, his hooded gaze taking in Nikki again. "I dropped her suitcase in my room where Kitten put her."

"You have no business in here," Patricia chided her as if Nikki were a child in a china cabinet. "If Travers caught you in here…"

"He gave me permission to—"

"He shouldn't have done that." Patricia motioned frantically for Nikki to leave. "This room, this entire wing, is off-limits. I've had your things moved downstairs to the pool house."

"The pool house?" Cull said with an arch of one eyebrow.

Nikki shot him a puzzled look as she tried to understand why he seemed amused by this.

Cull shook his head in disapproval at his stepmother. "The pool house will allow her to have the run of the entire ranch while the rest of us are asleep in our beds."

"Well, what did you expect me to do with her?" Patricia demanded. "Your father wouldn't hear of putting her up in a motel in town or better yet sending her back where she came from."

Nikki wanted to remind them that she was still in the room. "I'm sorry. I didn't mean to cause any trouble."

"Oh, please," Patricia said, spinning on her heels. "*Everyone* knows what you're really about. You aren't the first one who's come here wanting to satisfy your morbid curiosity."

"I hope to help."

The woman's laugh could have shattered crystal. *"Help?"* She seemed to be choking on laughter. "You've thrown the entire house into turmoil. You call this helping?"

Nikki could feel Cull's keen gaze on her. She rubbed at the painful spot on her temple, still surprised she'd hit as hard as she had. She really was lucky she hadn't been hurt worse or killed.

"Cull will show you to the pool house after dinner." With that, Patricia made a rude sound and stormed away.

Her leaving the room, though, didn't cool the heated anger in it. Nikki could feel it coming off Cull in waves.

"This must give you great pleasure, this front-row seat into our family drama," Cull said through clenched teeth.

"The kidnapping has been a lot of stress on your family for twenty-five years," she pointed out.

He smiled at that. "You think?" His intense blue gaze seemed to drill into her skull as he locked eyes with her. "You know all about us, though, don't you? I suspect you knew who I was when you stepped in front of my pickup. That you've known everything about this family for some time."

She lifted her chin a little higher. There was no reason to deny it. He'd seen through her stunt. She could have mentally kicked herself. Hadn't she known that Cull was the wrong person to cross?

"You know so much about us and yet we know so little about you," he was saying. "It makes me wonder why you chose our...tragedy for a book." When she didn't respond, he continued. "Well, seems you're going to be our guest for a while. Until you get what you need." His deep, soft voice reverberated through her. While Ledger had seemed impossibly young and innocent, Cull was anything but. This was a man not to be fooled with.

"But I have to wonder what a woman like

you needs," he finished, his voice so low and so seductive that it felt like a deep, dark well drawing her in. "I have to wonder just how far you will go."

Nikki swallowed and asked, "Has anyone been staying in the pool house? I don't want to put them out of their lodgings."

Cull's smile filled her with dread. "The pool house has been empty since the night of the kidnapping. It's where an item from one of the twins' beds was found. Apparently, the kidnapper and accomplice met there before at least one of them disappeared with the twins."

A chill rattled through her. Nikki hugged herself. That information hadn't been in *any* of the research she'd done on the case. It was the kind of thing that the FBI held back. What item had been found in the place where she would be staying? That meant that at least one of the kidnappers had been in that building that night. Her father? Marianne? Or someone in this house right now?

"You should be quite comfortable there since the place has its own set of ghosts," Cull assured her. "It's far enough away from the house that you won't be able to hear my father and stepmother arguing and yet no one will hear you should you run into trouble and need help. I'll try not to be too far away though. For your own sake. Wouldn't want you to have another...*accident*. How is your head by the way?"

She ignored the sarcasm laced with accusation. "The aspirin helped, thank you." Picking Cull had definitely been a mistake. Why had she thought he would be more helpful to her if he thought he'd almost killed her? From the look in his eye, he was wishing he hadn't braked.

"So you and your brothers live..."

"I would imagine you saw our cabins from the twins' window."

She had seen what looked like cabins set back in the trees some distance from the house. "You really are afraid of the ghosts," she only half joked.

His handsome face grew serious. "You think I'm joking? We'll see how you feel in a few days."

Chapter Eight

As Nikki and Cull descended the stairs, Ledger came out of his father's office.

"I don't believe you've met our houseguest," Cull said to his brother. "This is Ms. Nikki St. James, the famous true crime writer."

Ledger had clearly already heard about her, Nikki thought. He shook her hand warily.

"Patty has decided our guest would be more comfortable in the pool house," Cull said.

Ledger looked surprised, but added, "Whatever makes Patty happy."

"I need to make a quick call. Why don't you show Nikki to the dining room," Cull said.

"I'm glad we finally get to meet," she told the young man.

"You realize we're all shocked that our father would hire you."

"He didn't hire me. He's just giving me access to the ranch and the family so I can write about the kidnapping and hopefully uncover what really happened that night. I hope you'll help me."

Ledger let out a nervous laugh. "Me? I can't imagine how I could help. I was three."

"You might be surprised what you remember," she said, making him appear even more nervous. She quickly changed the subject. "I'm afraid I've upset your stepmother."

"Don't worry about it," he said as they walked toward the back of the house. "She's often upset over something."

"She caught me in the nursery."

He slowed so he studied her. "Oh. No one is allowed in that wing except the housekeeper, and even Tilly hates to go in there. The nursery is exactly as it was twenty-five years ago. My father insisted it be left that way. At first so that no evidence was lost. He was convinced that the FBI and local law enforcement would find the twins. Later it was left because he couldn't bear to change it."

"How awful for your family."

"Yes," he agreed as they reached the dining room. "Not to mention the glare of the media over the years. You can't believe the extremes some reporters will go to in an attempt to get a story."

She felt her face heat at his words.

"That's why I'm surprised my father opened the doors to you. Here we are," he said.

Stepping through the dining room doorway ahead of Ledger, she saw that Patricia and Travers were having a muted discussion in the far corner. At the center of the room was a huge cherrywood table and chairs that seemed to dwarf the large room. Kitten was already seated, and so were two men she didn't recognize.

Nikki felt a draft move across the back of her neck and shivered as it quilled the tiny hairs. She turned, expecting… Not sure what she expected to see. One of the ghosts?

THAT NIGHT AT DINNER, the sheriff told her husband about the woman who Cull McGraw had nearly run down. "I think it was staged. Too much of a coincidence that she steps in front of a McGraw pickup when she's on her way to the house anyway. But unfortunately, no one in the café saw anything."

"You have a very suspicious mind," Luke said, looking up from his meal. "What do you think she's after?"

"Supposedly, she's there to write a book about the McGraw kidnapping for the twenty-fifth anniversary."

"That sounds reasonable. I'm sure you checked her out."

McCall nodded. "She was born Nikki Ann Corwin."

"Corwin—why does that name ring a bell?"

"Because her father was Nate Corwin, the man who was convicted of the kidnapping," she said. "I can't help but wonder if Travers McGraw knows that."

"No wonder you're suspicious." He reached over onto Tracey's high chair to drop more finely chopped beef roast. She'd named her daughter after her father, Trace Winchester.

Tracey beat the high-chair tray with her spoon for a moment before laughing, then, ignoring the spoon, began eating the beef with the fingers of her free hand.

McCall smiled at her daughter. She never got tired of watching her, fascinated by the simple things the child did. She'd been so afraid of motherhood and hadn't admitted it until she was nine months pregnant.

Luke had talked her into taking a three-month leave while she decided if she wanted to be a stay-at-home mother or keep her job as sheriff.

"It's whatever you want," he'd told her. "I know you can do both. It's up to you."

McCall was glad she'd taken the time off. She loved being with her baby, but she also loved her job. She'd been afraid he was wrong and she really couldn't have both.

"I think I might drive out to the Sundown Stallion Station in the morning," she said as she straightened her daughter's bib and was rewarded with a huge toothy smile.

Being a game warden with the Fish, Wildlife and Parks Department, Luke was trained and served as an officer of the law. She didn't have to tell him why this year in particular, the McGraw kidnapping was on her mind.

"I have the day off tomorrow," he said. "Pepper's invited us out for lunch. Ruby's going, too."

McCall lifted a brow in surprise. "My mother and grandmother at lunch together? We need to get Tracey a bulletproof vest."

He chuckled as he rose to pull their daughter out of her high chair. "Probably a good idea."

The sheriff had to smile. That her mother and grandmother could be in the same room together and not kill each other was nothing short of amazing. For years Pepper Winchester hadn't acknowledged that McCall was even her granddaughter because of her dislike for Ruby.

Ruby had married Pepper's favorite son. Pepper had believed that Ruby had trapped Trace by getting pregnant and had wanted nothing to do with her—or the baby she had been carrying. Until a few years ago, McCall hadn't known anything about that side of her family, since her father had disappeared before she was born.

She'd never even laid eyes on her grandmother who'd become a recluse after Trace's disappearance. Nor had she known why Pepper Winchester wanted nothing to do with her. Her mother, Ruby, certainly hadn't been a wealth of information.

Then McCall, who'd been working as a deputy back then, had stumbled onto an old shallow grave. In the grave was proof of her father's identity. Everyone had thought that he'd left town, run out on her and her mother. Finding his remains had brought more than his murder to light.

It had opened up a world to her that had always been a mystery. McCall would never forget the first time she'd seen the Winchester Ranch—let alone met her grandmother Pepper. It had changed all of their lives.

"Give my regards to Pepper tomorrow," she said now. "I'm sure she understands why I can't make lunch."

"Your grandmother loves that you're sheriff. You know she would have been disappointed if you had quit."

McCall did know that. She just hoped her grandmother didn't have an ulterior motive for inviting them to lunch. It wouldn't be the first time Pepper had something going on that she didn't want the law involved in.

As her husband began to get their daughter ready for bed, McCall felt a shiver. Just the thought of the kidnapping sent a spike of cold terror through her. She couldn't imagine losing her daughter. It was no wonder Marianne McGraw had lost her mind and was now locked away in the mental hospital.

McCall had been a child herself at the time of the kidnapping, but she'd heard stories about it and read both the newspaper accounts as well as the police file on it.

The FBI had been called in almost at once and taken over the case, but from what she'd read about the investigation, there had been several suspects, including the babies' own mother, Marianne. But it had always seemed that the dalliance between the stable manager, Nate Corwin, and Marianne McGraw had been conjecture without any solid evidence.

The person who'd testified about the affair had been the nanny, Patricia Owens—now Travers McGraw's second wife.

It was speculated that Nate and Marianne had come up with the kidnapping of the twins for the ransom money. Nate Corwin was a mere horse trainer. Marianne had no money of her own. What they'd planned to do with the twins after they collected the ransom was unknown since neither had confessed. Marianne had gone into shock. Nate had denied his involvement right up until his death.

McCall knew what it was like to fall so deeply in love that you could lose all perspective. But she shuddered at the thought that a mother would jeopardize the lives of her babies for money and a man. Any man.

TRAVERS SAW NIKKI as she entered the dining room, and said something quietly to his wife before greeting her. "I don't believe you've met our attorney. Jim Waters, this is the woman I told you about," Travers said.

The attorney was fiftysomething with thinning brown hair and small brown eyes. He turned awkwardly, a deep frown burrowing between his brows, and held out his hand. His handshake was limp and slightly damp, and his eyes didn't meet hers.

"And this is Blake Ryan, our former ranch manager and a close friend."

Blake was about the same age as the other man, but unlike Waters, he was distinguished and cover-model handsome. His dark hair had grayed at the temples, bringing out the steel of his gray eyes. His handshake was strong and he met her gaze with both suspicion and wariness.

"Why don't you sit over here by me," Travers said to her after making the introductions. He didn't need to tell her that both men had some concerns about her being here.

She'd just sat down when she heard the sound of boot soles on the wood floor. She sensed rather than saw Cull enter the dining room because she kept her gaze averted. She didn't glance over at him as he took a chair next to his father, directly across from her.

Suddenly the room felt too small. She took a shallow breath and dared to look at him. His gaze was on her, those blue eyes drilling her to her chair.

Ledger had taken a seat down the table next to Kitten, who looked far too happy, all things considered, since she hadn't gotten to go into town yet.

Nikki tried to relax but the tension in the dining room was dense enough to smother her. Patricia had lowered herself into her chair at the end of the table with a sullen dignity, only to glare down the length of it at her husband.

Boone was the last brother to come in. She hadn't met him yet because he'd been out of town picking up a horse, she'd heard. He stopped in the doorway. He could have been Cull's twin.

He had the same thick dark hair, the same intense blue eyes, the same broad shoulders, the same scowl.

"What's going on?" Boone asked as if feeling the tension in the air before his gaze lit on her.

Travers got to his feet. "Please sit down, son." He waited for Boone to take a chair before he said, "This is Nikki St. James. She's a true crime writer and will be investigating the kidnapping for a book. I want you all to cooperate with her."

"Like hell." Boone shoved back his chair and stood, towering over the table. "I'm sorry, Dad, but this was a huge mistake. I'm not having anything to do with this…book or—" he turned his gaze on Nikki "—or this woman." With that he stomped out.

"I apologize for my son," Travers said wearily.

"You don't have to do that," she said as she heard the front door slam and the sound of an engine rev after it. "I know how hard this is on your family." She glanced around the table. She could feel Cull's gaze on her. Like Boone, he didn't want her here.

Kitten was giving her that snotty look she'd apparently perfected. Her mother's steely blue gaze could have burned through sheet metal.

Ledger was the only one who gave her a slight smile as if he felt sorry for her.

"I will try to make it as painless as I can, but I need all of your help if I have any chance of solving this," she finished.

"Solving it?" Patricia said with a snort, but quickly reverted her gaze to her plate as her husband gave her an impatient look.

"I'll speak to Boone," Travers said. "I should have told him about this. He doesn't do well with surprises." Though Boone had been only five when the twins were kidnapped, he might still have memories of that night.

"I should help Frieda." Patricia got up and went into the kitchen. A few moments later, she returned with the cook, who was carrying a large tray full of small bowls of soup. Patricia put a bowl in front of Travers and another in front of Cull before she sat down. Frieda placed soup in front of Patricia, then worked her way around the table until she came to Nikki. For a moment, she looked confused. "I guess I left yours in the kitchen," the cook said.

"Let me," Kitten said, jumping up and hurrying after her.

The two returned moments later. Kitten, all smiles, put a bowl of soup in front of Nikki before sitting down again.

"Thank you, Kitten," Travers said, smiling at

the teen, though looking surprised she would get up to help.

Cook placed two large plates of sandwiches in the center of the table and left.

Nikki picked up her spoon. Steam rose from the soup. She caught a scent she didn't recognize. Kitten leaned behind Waters to whisper, "Aren't you afraid it might be poisoned?"

Normally she had a good appetite. Even without Kitten taunting her, she wasn't that hungry. She started to dip her spoon into the soup, when Cull reached across the table and switched bowls with her. He gave his stepsister a challenging look. Kitten rolled her eyes and waited for him to take a bite.

"What is going on?" Patricia demanded.

"It seems Kitten thinks Nikki's soup may be poisoned," Cull said. The man had remarkably good hearing. Or he knew Kitten too well.

"What?" Patricia seemed beside herself.

Kitten gave her a shrug as if she had no idea what Cull was talking about.

"This is ridiculous," Patricia said, and started to get up. But before she could, Travers reached over and switched bowls with Cull.

"Kitten, I will speak with you later," he said. He picked up his spoon and took a sip of the soup.

"I didn't do anything," the teen whined, and

glared over at her brother who hadn't touched his soup.

Travers started to take a second spoonful, when he suddenly dropped his spoon. It hit the edge of the bowl. The sound was startling in the silent room. Everyone looked in his direction as he clutched his chest, his eyes wide and terrified before he toppled to the floor.

Chapter Nine

Cull studied the toes of his boots. Anything to keep him from looking at Nikki St. James sitting a seat away from the family in the hospital waiting room.

If his fool stepsister had tried to poison the woman… He glanced at Kitten. She was sulking in the corner. On the way to the hospital, all of them piled in Patricia's Suburban, Kitten had continued to protest that she hadn't poisoned Nikki's soup, that she'd just been teasing and that maybe the cook had done it.

Finally, Cull had told her to keep quiet, at which point Patricia had gone off on all of them for mistreating Kitten. "She's as upset as the rest of you and she's just a child!"

Cull had concentrated on the road ahead, determined not to get into it with any of them. They'd followed the ambulance to the hospital and were told to wait.

Earlier Ledger had gotten everyone coffee. Cull had watched him ask Nikki if she wanted some. She'd volunteered to go with him to the machine. After hearing how it was that Cull had brought her to the ranch, Ledger had accused him of "literally running her down on Main Street."

Since then Ledger had been especially nice to the crime writer in spite of Cull telling him that he didn't trust the woman. He could see what Nikki was up to and he planned to put an end to it once they were alone.

At the sound of footfalls, Cull looked up—as did the rest of them—and saw Boone storming in. *"What happened?"* he demanded. He had beer on his breath, which answered the question as to where he'd gone after he'd stomped out earlier.

"We don't know for sure—" Cull didn't get to finish.

"Someone poisoned Dad," Ledger said. "At least that's what we think happened."

"Poisoned him?"

"We don't know for sure," Cull said.

Patricia jumped to her feet. "This is all her fault," she accused, pointing a finger at Nikki. "It was her bowl of soup—"

Boone shot a look at Nikki.

"Hold on, everyone," Cull said, raising his

hands as they all started talking at once. "Nikki was the intended *victim*. Perhaps, Patricia, you should be talking to your daughter. She was the one who brought the bowl of soup out of the kitchen."

Patricia sputtered as if unable to get the words out fast enough. "*Kitten?* Kitten wouldn't... How can you possibly think..."

"I was just teasing." Kitten burst into tears and ran from the waiting room.

"Now see what you've done?" Patricia demanded before she went after her daughter.

"Let's all just calm down," Cull said. "I called the sheriff when we got here. I'm sure McCall will be able to—" He stopped as he saw the doctor and the sheriff coming down the hall toward him. Heart in his throat, he waited, fearing what the news was going to be.

NIKKI WATCHED THE two come down the hall. She couldn't tell from their somber faces what they'd discovered. If Travers had been poisoned... Her stomach knotted at the thought. Was there someone in this family *that* determined to keep her from learning the truth? What if because of her, Travers McGraw lost his life? She couldn't bear the thought.

Boone started to speak, but the sheriff cut him off. "Your father wasn't poisoned."

Nikki felt a wave of relief wash over her. She'd been so afraid that Kitten had done something stupid in an attempt to get rid of her.

"He's had a heart attack," the doctor said. "He's in stable condition, but not out of the woods yet. Were any of you aware of your father's heart problems?"

The attorney, who'd been sitting at the edge of the group, spoke for the first time. "Travers knew he had a bad ticker?" Jim Waters asked.

The doctor nodded. "I've warned him how important it was for him to relieve stress and eat healthy and slow down. I had hoped he might have shared that information with his family."

Cull groaned. "It was just like him not to."

"I want to see him," Boone said.

"If anyone should get to see him, it should be me," Patricia said as she came down the hall.

The doctor held up his hands. "None of you are going to see him. Right now the last thing he needs is more…stress." As Patricia started to argue, the doctor said, "You will be able to see him possibly in the morning, but only one at a time. And I won't have *any* of you upsetting him."

They all fell silent for a moment before Cull said, "You heard him. Dad's in stable condition. Let's all go home."

Nikki's head ached. She couldn't wait to get back to the ranch and take a couple of aspirin.

"I'm not riding with *you*," Kitten announced to Cull. "I'm riding with Boone."

Patricia took her daughter's hand. "No one's leaving until you all apologize to my daughter."

Cull let out a curse. "An apology? Have you forgotten that no one would have thought that Dad had been poisoned if it wasn't for Kitten? Fortunately the doctor recognized his condition as a heart attack, otherwise they would have been pumping his stomach while he was dying of heart failure."

"All that matters is that Dad is going to be all right. But this constant bickering has to stop," Ledger said.

"Then get rid of *her*!" Patricia said, pointing again at Nikki. "Now with Travers in the hospital, the whole idea of a book on the kidnapping should be scrapped."

"Patricia's right," Boone said, speaking up. "You just heard what the doctor said. Dad doesn't need the stress of having someone digging up the past, and for no reason, since we all know who kidnapped the twins."

Cull shook his head. "This isn't the time or the place to discuss this, and if any one of you dare bring this up when you see Dad…" He saw from their faces that they got the message. "In the meantime, Nikki stays and does whatever it is she does. If Dad changes his mind, *he'll* send her packing—but not us and not before Dad is well enough to make that call. Boone, I'm going to take your pickup. You can ride in Patricia's Suburban since you've obviously been drinking. Nikki, you come with me. The rest of you can go with Patricia or walk, I don't care." He reached for Nikki. "Let's go."

CULL GRIPPED THE steering wheel so hard he was white-knuckled as they left the hospital.

"Thank you for sticking up for me back at the hospital," Nikki said once they were on the road headed toward the ranch.

"I didn't do it for you," Cull said through gritted teeth without looking at her. "I did it for my father."

Out of the corner of his eye, he saw her turn away to look out her side window. Open prairie ran for miles, broken only occasionally by farmland all the way to the Little Rockies. He loved this country. Where some people saw nothing, he saw the beauty of the wild grasses, the rolling landscape, the huge sky overhead that ran from horizon to horizon, living up to the name Big Sky Country.

The night was clear and cool. Stars glittered in a canopy of navy velvet. He rolled down his window as they left town behind. The smell of sage and dust and wild grasses filled his nostrils. He breathed it in and tried to calm down. This was home. The prairie soothed him in a way no other landscape ever had. He loved this part of Montana the way others loved the mountains and pine trees.

For a moment, he wondered what Nikki saw when she looked out there. Or did she yearn for towering mountains studded with pine trees? He'd found few women who appreciated his part of the state. It was one reason he'd never settled down.

"I feel responsible for what's happened," she said. "I'm so glad your father is going to be all right."

He glanced over at her, his expression softening when he saw the tears in her eyes. "It's not your fault. Dad hasn't been well. You heard what the doctor said. The anniversary of the kidnapping is just one more weight piled onto all the stress he's normally under."

"I'm sorry," she said. "I wish there was some way I could help. If my leaving would help..."

He slowed for the turn into the ranch. "You would give up that easily? I thought you were determined to find out the truth about the kidnapping?"

"I am, but I can't promise—"

Cull laughed. "*Now* you play coy?" He shook his head. "Sorry, I'm not buying it. I think you'd do anything to get this particular story and that makes me wonder about you."

"What you see is what you get," she said, then added quickly, "You know what I mean."

He smiled. "You would have eaten that soup, wouldn't you?"

"Yes. Why does that bother you?" she asked.

Cull scoffed. "Because it shows me the kind of woman you are. You don't back down."

"I'm going to take that as a compliment."

"Suit yourself." He could feel her gaze on him as he pulled up in front of the house and parked.

"You know what I think? I think the reason you and the others are frightened of my digging into the kidnapping is because you have something to hide. There's something you held back all those years ago. Maybe it's just a memory that has haunted you. A sound, something that was said, something that you saw but didn't understand at the time."

He wanted to tell her how crazy she was, but she'd gotten too close to the truth. But some secrets were best kept silent, since they wouldn't change the kidnapping. Nor would they change who'd been behind it. "That's what you're counting on to solve this? Good luck."

"I was hoping that all of you would want this solved as much as your father does," she said.

Cull turned off the engine and turned to face her. "You just don't get it. We've been living with this for twenty-five years. Do you have any idea how painful all this is for us to have to relive every year? Can't you now see that it's killing my father?"

"That's why he needs to know what really happened."

Cull shook his head as he took off his Stetson and raked a hand through his hair. A dark lock fell over his eyes before he shoved the hat back on. For a moment, he simply studied her, wanting to look deeper, clear to her soul. If she hadn't already sold it for a story.

"I swear this tops it all. A *true crime writer*? And I thought the psychic he hired was bad enough."

"The sooner I can get to work, the sooner I will be gone."

He cocked his head, narrowing his eyes. "Gone, but not forgotten."

She seemed to ignore that and met his gaze with a steely one of her own.

"Why? What does it matter to you? I'm sure there are other tragic stories for you to delve into out there. So what is it about our particular story?"

Nikki looked away, giving him the impression that for some reason this time it was more than finding out the truth for a bestseller. Again he found himself wondering, *Who is this woman?*

All his instincts told him that she was hiding something but he couldn't for the life of him figure out what it was. She was already a *New York Times* bestselling author. From what he could tell, she didn't need the money or the attention. She'd already made a name for herself. Writing another book about some horrendous crime wasn't going to get her anything she didn't already have.

Or would it?

"I'm not sure what you're after," he said carefully. "But I saw the way you were with my brother. You're not using Ledger to get whatever it is you're really after. Right now because of another woman who took him for a ride, he doesn't know his ass from a teakettle. You stay away from him. He was too young to remember anything about the kidnapping. I won't have you using him."

"I'm not using your brother."

Cull scoffed. "And you just happened to be in Whitehorse today sitting across from the café where my brother has breakfast on the days his ex-girlfriend waitresses there."

He caught her moment of surprise before she

carefully hid it. "That's right," he said with a bitter chuckle. "For whatever reason, you will do whatever you have to, use whoever you have to, tear this family apart to get what you want." He frowned as he studied her. "For a book? I don't think so. Just know that while you're digging into every dark corner of our lives, I'm going to be digging into yours. I can't wait to find out what your real story is, Nikki St. James."

With that he opened his door and climbed out. He heard her open her door and exit, as well. A set of headlights washed over him as Patricia pulled the Suburban up in the yard.

Cull was in no mood for any of them. He didn't bother going inside, but instead took the path beside the house and headed for the stables. He was breathing hard, sucking in the cold night air as he tried to cool his anger. Chill down the heat that filled him whenever he got around that woman. Nikki St. James rattled him more than he wanted to admit. No good could come of this for any of them. He had to find a way to get rid of her and soon.

NIKKI STOOD NEXT to the ranch pickup feeling as if she'd just gone three rounds in the ring. Cull suspected there was more to her story for being here. He hadn't found it. Not yet, but he suspected enough that he wouldn't stop until he discovered the truth about her.

She let out a humorless chuckle. He said she wouldn't stop at anything? He was just like her. She watched him take off and realized he'd left her not so she could deal with his family, but so he could escape all of them.

"He's not usually so...rude."

Nikki spun around to find Ledger standing right behind her. "You startled me."

"Sorry." Ledger glanced toward the rest of his family entering the house. Patricia was arguing with Kitten about something as they started up the porch steps. Nikki was reminded of earlier when the teen almost knocked her down the stairs.

Jim Waters and Blake Ryan both walked past without looking at her. Patricia stopped on the porch and called down, "I'll get cook to put sandwiches out. I don't know about the rest of you, but I'm starved." Her gaze lit on Nikki. She turned quickly and went into the house.

"I heard that Patricia moved you out of the wing upstairs and put your belongings in the pool house," Ledger said. "Why don't I go with you to make sure everything is ready for you?"

"Thank you. That would be nice," she said, happy to have some time alone with Ledger. She was reminded, though, of what Cull said about not using his brother. "But Cull might not approve. He's worried that I'll take advantage of you."

Ledger chuckled. "Cull's the oldest so he always thinks he has to protect us all. His heart is in the right place, though."

"Why do you think he feels he needs to protect you from me?" she asked innocently enough as they walked down a path that led around the house.

"He thinks I'm a fool."

"Because of the woman at the café," she said as they left the house behind and walked through a stand of aspens. "I was sitting across the street this morning. I couldn't help but notice."

His smile was sad. "Abby."

The darkness felt good. So did being around Ledger. There was a quiet confidence about him that was nice, especially after the intensity of his older brother. "You're in love with her."

"It's that obvious, huh?" He laughed. "I guess Cull's right. I'm pretty transparent. He thinks I should forget her." He shrugged. "Can't."

"You're worried about her."

"With good reason. Her husband is…" He waved his hand through the air as if he couldn't come up with a name that was appropriate in front of her.

"But she won't leave him."

"Nope," he said with a shake of his head. She could hear the frustration in his words. "She says he needs her. I don't get it."

Nikki said nothing. There was nothing she could say. Women often stayed with controlling men for their own reasons. Who knew what Abby's real reason was.

"What do you remember about the night of the kidnapping?"

He glanced over at her, clearly a little taken aback by the quick change of subject. But she also noticed that his guard had gone up.

"I told you, I was three."

"Oh, I thought you might be able to help, especially given your father's health. I want to find out the truth for him more than ever now."

He nodded, looking guilty. "I think I remember…little things. Waking up to hear Patty screaming. The sound of people running down the hallway toward the nursery. My father on the phone to the sheriff. But I've heard my brothers say the same thing over the years, so maybe they are actually their memories and not even mine. There is one memory that I think is mine because when I think about that night I see myself standing at the end of the hall until someone noticed me."

"Who noticed you?"

"Patty. She was our nanny then."

"Did she say anything?"

"I'm sure I asked her what was going on." He shrugged. "I have a faint memory of her saying something about making pancakes in the morning. See, I really have nothing that could help."

Pancakes? That sounded like a very strange conversation, if that's what it had been.

Ledger stopped in front of a small building. Next to it was a large swimming pool. The breeze ruffled the surface of the water, making it lap at the edges. He looked back at the house. Golden light spilled from most of the windows as if all the lights had been turned on.

"What if you find out who kidnapped Oakley and Jesse Rose only to discover that they're dead?"

"I think not knowing is worse for your father. Maybe if the truth came out, it would let everyone heal."

He shook his head. "Dad lives with hope. If you take that away…"

In the silence that fell between them, she heard voices coming from the back porch. Two figures were silhouetted there against the lights coming from the house. One was clearly Patricia. The other was a man, but she couldn't be sure who.

She turned, trying to catch their words on

the breeze. Behind her, she heard Ledger open the door to the pool house. A moment later, a bright light came on.

"There you go," Ledger said in a voice loud enough that it would carry to the back of the house. "If you need anything, just holler."

The voices silenced. She turned to look at Ledger, surprised to realize that he'd signaled Patricia and whoever she'd been in an intense conversation with that they weren't alone. When Nikki looked back, the two figures had bled into the shadows and were gone.

Cull was so sure that she had Ledger wrapped around her little finger. That he would do anything she asked. That he would let her use him.

As Ledger met her gaze, she saw something in his eyes before they darted away that gave her a start. Ledger was just as protective of the McGraw secrets as his brother Cull.

They were definitely hiding something, but she couldn't be sure it had anything to do with the kidnapping. What had the boys seen or heard that night that they were afraid she was going to uncover? Was there a secret they'd been keeping all these years? But if true, *who* were they protecting?

Glancing toward the stables, she thought she saw a figure standing just inside out of the light. Cull? Over her shoulder, she said to Ledger, "I know there is something you're all keeping from me. What I don't understand is why."

There was no answer. When she looked back, she saw that he was headed for the house. He appeared to be in a hurry.

Seeing her suitcase waiting for her just inside, she pushed open the door to the pool house. The place was beautifully furnished. As it hadn't been used since the kidnapping, she had to assume that Marianne was the one who'd decorated not only the pool house but the main house, as well.

She would be quite comfortable here instead of Cull's former room on the haunted wing, she thought, even though this small building might have even more persistent ghosts. Why, though, did Patricia want her out of the house so badly?

Before she walked through the door, she glanced again toward the house.

Her pulse jumped, her heart taking off like the wild stallion Boone had brought home earlier. Someone was standing at a second-story window. Her chest constricted as she realized that the window was at the end of the south wing. Someone had been watching her and Ledger from the nursery.

A shock wave moved through her as she saw the figure was a woman dressed in all white.

Even her hair appeared to be white. For just a heartbeat, she thought it was Marianne.

The breeze billowed the curtains. Nikki blinked and the figure was gone as if she'd only imagined it—unlike the chill that moved through her, turning her blood to ice.

Chapter Ten

Patricia called from the back porch saying cook had set out the sandwiches as Nikki started to close the pool house door. She felt her stomach growl. They'd missed lunch and now it was way past dinner.

"I can bring you a sandwich if you'd rather not go back to the house tonight."

She saw Cull come out of the darkness on the path from the barn. "I'm not that hun—" Her stomach growled again. By then, he'd reached her. He grinned, clearly having heard her stomach, and turned toward the house. "I'll be right back."

"Thank you, but I hate to have you go if you aren't hungry."

Cull stopped to look back at her. "If you want to eat by the pool, I'll bring back enough for both of us. Then we can talk."

She nodded, although she wasn't sure she

liked the sound of that. Had Travers called and told him to send her packing? Or was Cull willing to help her with the book?

Nikki had yet to step inside the pool house, where she would be staying. She did so now, then picked up her suitcase and carried it into the bedroom.

It had been a long day. All she could think about was climbing into the bed and sleeping. But even as she thought it, she wondered how much sleep she would be able to get. So much had happened today and her list of suspects just seemed to continue to grow.

Not to mention the fact that she was starving.

Hearing a tap at the open door a few minutes later, she looked up to find Cull standing there. He had a tray with sandwiches, glasses of milk and cake. Chocolate cake. Her stomach growled loudly.

"Let's get you fed," he said, motioning toward the pool rather than coming inside. She'd been surprised that the McGraws had a pool since it was so seasonal in Montana. She said as much as she joined him at the outdoor table.

"My mother loved to swim. Now Kitten enjoys it. I take a dip occasionally." He handed her a plate with several sandwich options.

"But no one uses the pool house?"

"My mother used to come down here and

read when she needed a break from all of us," Cull said. "It was her...sanctuary." He seemed to remember that the kidnappers had possibly met here that night before the twins were whisked off, never to be seen again. His expression soured.

Nikki wanted to ask him questions about his mother but right now seemed the wrong time. She took a bite of one of the quartered sandwiches. Chicken salad. It tasted wonderful.

"How is your father?" she asked after she'd swallowed.

He didn't seem surprised that she would know he'd call the hospital after they got back. "Resting comfortably, the doctor said."

Nikki took another bite and noticed that Cull hadn't touched his yet. He was watching her.

"What?" she asked as she finished and picked up another.

"You. I'm used to women who don't eat carbs. Hell, don't eat anything, from what I can tell." For a moment, she wanted to defend her eating habits and her rounded though slim figure. He didn't give her a chance. "I like women who have curves."

Cull seemed to realize what he'd said. "I mean—" He laughed softly and picked up a sandwich. "I should just shut up and eat, huh."

They ate in a companionable silence for a

while. He'd turned on the pool lights. The water shimmered invitingly.

"You're welcome to go in," he said, clearly having noticed the longing in her expression.

"I didn't bring a suit."

"I wouldn't let that stop you."

She laughed at that. "I've already caused a stir around here. I can well imagine what your stepmother would say."

"Yes, Patty." He shook his head. "Life is strange, isn't it?"

"Do you remember her when she was your nanny?"

He nodded thoughtfully. "Quiet, shy, mousy, I think is how the press described her. I've often wondered about the change in her." He eyed her closely. "I'm sure you do, too."

She met his gaze for a moment before she lowered hers and hesitated as she looked at the chocolate cake.

Cull picked up a piece and put it in front of her. "Enjoy—you deserve it after the day you've had."

"I could say the same to you."

He nodded and looked toward the pool. "I'm sorry I gave you such a hard time earlier."

"Speaking of earlier, I heard Patty talking to someone behind the house. It sounded rather heated."

"I think it was Blake. He's been with Dad

from as far back as I can remember. They were probably arguing over Dad's health. Blake thinks Patty could be more...agreeable."

Nikki wondered if Cull really expected her to believe that's what they were arguing about. She hadn't been able to make out much of the argument but it hadn't been about Travers's health. And she suspected Cull knew that, since the barn was closer to the house—and the argument.

"I really doubt that was what they were arguing about and you know it," she said, calling him on it. "Why lie about it? What is it you're all trying so hard to keep from me?"

He looked up at her in surprise, his gaze suddenly calculating. "You don't miss much."

"It's my job," she said defensively.

"For the book."

There was that suspicion again. She felt her heart quicken—from his look, from his words. "I know it's hard. A stranger coming in who might uncover your most intimate secrets. It's hard for me, too. I often get emotionally involved with the family. I'm human. But I'm not here to hurt any of you. I just want—"

"The truth." He nodded as if he still had his doubts about her real reasons as he rose from his chair. "You look as if you are going to fall asleep right out here by the pool." He removed the other piece of chocolate cake from the tray and picked up the dirty dishes. "I'll take these up to the house. The cake...well, you might wake up in the middle of the night and need something."

It was such a sweet gesture, bringing down the sandwiches, eating with her out here by the pool, leaving the cake and taking the dirty dishes. She couldn't help but be touched. "Thank you."

"I'm sure I'll see you in the morning. Breakfast is at seven but if that is too early for you, Frieda will see that you get whatever you need." He seemed to hesitate for a moment as if there was more he wanted to say. But then he smiled almost sadly and said, "Good night, Nikki. Sleep well."

"So that's what's going on," Patricia said the moment Cull pushed open the door to the kitchen and put down the tray. "Conspiring with the enemy."

He shook his head. It was late and he was too exhausted from the day he'd had to argue with her. "Let's not get into it." He started to turn away, but she grabbed his arm.

"Your father is lying in a hospital bed and it is all that woman's fault!"

He turned to face her. "*No, it's not.* If anyone is to blame, it's you. You harp and harp at him until I'm amazed he doesn't just tell you to shut the hell up."

Her eyes widened in shock. "How dare you—"

"Oh, I dare," he said, taking a step toward her. "I have been wanting to tell you how I feel for a very long time. My father took you in, married you and has helped raise your daughter and neither of you have ever said thank-you. You both just demand and demand. Nothing is ever enough."

She was shaking her head furiously. "You can't blame me for his heart attack. It's this stupid kidnapping. He just won't leave it alone."

Cull took a step back giving her an incredulous look. "*Stupid* kidnapping? Patty, his children were taken. For all he knows they're dead. Are you that self-centered that you can't understand that?"

She looked chastised for a moment, but quickly recovered. "Well, it's been twenty-five years. How long do you expect me to put up with this?"

"He is *never* going to forget. If you can't accept that, then there's the door. No one is forcing you and Kitten to stay here."

"You'd love to see that, wouldn't you?"

He said nothing, his earlier anger receding, leaving him feeling sorry for his harsh words, no matter how heartfelt. "Can't you just be happy?" He opened his arms to encompass not just the kitchen but the entire ranch. "Look where you live, look how you live. Can't you just embrace that?"

She sniffed and looked as if she might cry.

"And leave Nikki alone. Let her do what she came here to do."

"She's not going to find out anything more than the FBI and the sheriff did all those years ago." Something in her voice gave away her hope that that was the case. He'd often wondered if Patty had something to hide about the night of the kidnapping. If so, was she worried that Nikki would be able to uncover it? That could explain why she'd been so upset about the crime writer's appearance here.

"Only time will tell, I guess. I figure she'll be gone soon enough." He started to turn away again but this time it was her words that stopped him.

"Are you sure that's what you want?" There was accusation as well as mocking in her tone.

He stopped at the door, but didn't turn. "It's what we all want." And he was betting that each of them had their own reasons for wanting Nikki gone.

AFTER CULL LEFT, Nikki went inside the pool house, locking the doors before heading to the bedroom. She was so tired that she quickly brushed her teeth, stumbled into her pajamas and fell onto the bed.

She'd been so sure she wouldn't be able to sleep with everything that was going on. Everything including Cull. She thought of his intense blue eyes. He saw too much. But that meant he always had—even as a child. There was no doubt in her mind that he knew more about the kidnapping than he'd told anyone.

He was her last thought before she dropped into the deep, dark hole of sleep. That was why it took more than a few minutes for her to drag her way up and out of the dream.

She sat up in bed, rubbing her hands over her face as she tried to let go of what had started as a nice dream and had turned into a nightmare. Even as she thought it, she could feel the dream slipping away, leaving only that heavy, suffocating feeling of doom.

Nikki tried to hang on to the thread of her nightmare. Something to do with Cull and the horses in the barn and her father. She shook her head. Clearly not one of those dreams that made a lot of sense. She'd never even known her father. But he was in the dream. He was in the stables. And something horrible was happening.

That's when she woke up. She sat listening

to the night sounds. An owl hooted in the distance. Closer she heard a horse whinny. Then another horse, then another.

She frowned as she got out of bed and padded barefoot into the living area of the pool house to look out toward the stables. A light was on. She caught movement. Someone was in the horse barn.

Remnants of her nightmare made her heart beat faster. Maybe it hadn't been a dream. Maybe she'd heard something…

She opened the door. The Montana night was clear, the stars glittering overhead, only a slit of silver moon dangling over the barn. She made her way along the path, hugging herself against the slight chill in the air.

As she drew closer, she could hear the horses, restless in their stalls. A shadow moved along the edge of the horse barn. A moment later she heard raised voices. Male voices.

Her bare feet were beginning to ache from the cold of the stones along the path. She shivered, debating turning back. But curiosity won out. Her showing up at the ranch had caused a stir. If whoever was arguing in the barn this late at night had something to do with the kidnapping…

She moved to the edge of the barn door so

she could hear better over the whinnying and stomping of the horses inside.

"You're making a terrible mistake. If you're wrong…" She didn't recognize the male voice and wondered if it could be the former ranch manager who'd apparently been arguing with Patricia earlier.

"I know what I'm doing. I'll do whatever I have to." Her heart slammed against her rib cage. This voice she recognized. *Cull.*

"You said you don't want anyone to get hurt. I don't see how that can be avoided under the circumstances. This crime writer—"

"Don't worry. I'll take care of her myself if this all goes south."

Nikki felt the air rush from her lungs. She stumbled back, her shoulder hitting the gate. The metal latch rattled.

"Did you hear that?" the unfamiliar male voice asked a second before Nikki heard someone moving in her direction.

She flattened herself against the side of the barn but quickly realized she would be seen by whoever came out. Her only hope of getting away unseen was to go around the side of the building. But that meant climbing into the corral.

Nikki hurriedly climbed over the corral railing, dropping down to the soft hoof-turned earth. Her bare feet sunk into the dirt, slowing her escape. Just a few more yards and—

Suddenly out of the corner of her eye, she saw a horse come galloping out of the barn and into the corral. It headed right for her, ears back, hooves throwing up dirt clods as it barreled forward.

Nikki lunged for the corral fence as the huge horse bore down on her. Her hands brushed the railing and missed. Not that she would have been able to climb out before the horse reached her anyway.

Two strong, large hands grabbed her from around the waist and swung her up and over the railing. She felt the horse's breath at her neck. Before she knew what was happening, she slammed into a very solid male chest. Behind her, the horse stomped and snorted just feet away past the corral railing. She realized it must be the stallion that Boone had delivered to the ranch earlier.

The arms that had wrapped around her now set her down hard at the edge of the corral. *"What the hell do you think you're doing?"* Cull demanded as he held her at arm's length. "You could have been killed. What were you thinking getting into the corral?"

She couldn't speak and realized she was trembling all over from the close call. Worse, as she glanced toward the barn, she began trembling harder when she realized that someone had set that horse free in the corral. Cull? Then why save her?

"What are *you* doing out here?" she demanded.

"Checking the horses. I heard something."

She nodded. "So did I." She'd heard enough, that was for sure.

His gaze never left Nikki's face. He was studying her in the dim light from the barn as if he was trying to understand her. "You have no business in the corral. That's a wild horse in there."

She nodded and tried to swallow down the lump in her throat. Tears stung her eyes as she realized how close she'd come to being trampled. Worse, that she couldn't trust Cull.

He shook his head. She couldn't tell if he thought her silly and stupid. "Come on. I'll walk you back to the pool house."

She glanced toward the barn. The horses had settled back down. She saw no movement deep in the stalls. Whoever Cull had been talking to, he was gone. Which left the question of who had let the stallion out and why. Had he hoped to scare her? Or kill her?

She could smell Cull's very masculine scent intermingled with saddle leather and fresh air. If the purpose had been to scare her, then the stallion had done his job. She would have to be more careful, given what she'd overhead. Especially more careful when it came to Cull McGraw.

Chapter Eleven

Nikki drove into Whitehorse as the sun arced over the prairie. The day was beautiful, sunny and warm, the big sky blue and dotted with white fluffy clouds. She'd awoken before dawn with a suspicion that had felt like a douse of ice water.

She'd hurriedly done research on her phone before giving the sheriff a call and asking if she could come by and see her.

Sheriff McCall Crawford looked up from her desk as Nikki came in. She was a slim, pretty woman who Nikki had heard was a no-non-sense law officer. Mostly she'd heard that Mc-Call could be trusted.

"Thanks for seeing me," she said, and closed the door behind her.

The sheriff raised a brow. "You sounded so cryptic on the phone." She motioned to a chair and Nikki sat down. "I was planning to drive ut this morning to the ranch and see how you were doing."

"I'm sorry we met the way we did yesterday," Nikki said honestly. "Now I am hesitant to even voice my suspicions, but I hope you will take what I have to tell you seriously."

"Your suspicions after only one day at the Sundown Stallion Station? You really do work fast. I'm intrigued."

"Were you aware of Travers McGraw's health before his heart attack?"

"I'll admit I hadn't seen him in a good while," the sheriff said as she leaned back in her chair. "I was taken aback by his condition."

Nikki nodded. "His family seems to think the cause is his obsession with finding out what happened to the twins."

"But you don't think that's it?"

She shook her head. "I think he really *is* being poisoned." She pulled out her phone. "I've seen this once before. His symptoms are consistent with those of people who are being slowly exposed to small amounts of arsenic over time. Headaches, loss of weight, confusion, depression. In his case, finally cardiac arrest."

The sheriff looked skeptical. "I'm assuming you have no proof of this?"

"No, and I had the same reaction at first that

you are. But then I remembered that his wife Marianne had the same symptoms."

"Twenty-five years ago?" The sheriff sat up, leaning her elbows on her desk, definitely interested now.

"But in the same house. The same house *and* the same people living there," she said. "If I'm right, that would seem like too much of a coincidence, don't you think?"

"Marianne's depression was blamed on postpartum. Her other symptoms on possibly an illicit love affair."

Nikki nodded.

"No one else is experiencing these symptoms at the house?" the sheriff asked slowly, studying her.

"No, so I doubt it's tainted water or any other factor in the house causing it other than the obvious. Someone is intentionally poisoning him."

The sheriff said, "He's in the hospital. If he was being poisoned, it probably wouldn't still be in his system, except possibly in a strand of hair from his head."

Nikki nodded. It was one way to find out if there was any basis for her suspicion.

"Speaking of suspicion," the sheriff said, "how are you since your accident in front of the Whitehorse Café?"

"Fortunately, I wasn't hurt other than a knock on my head."

"Fortunately," the sheriff said, smiling.

Nikki got to her feet. "I won't keep you, but I was hoping you might see if my suspicions are valid. Given Travers McGraw's condition, I didn't think it was something that could wait."

"I suppose you have a suspect to go along with your suspicions?"

"It's a short list," Nikki said. "But I'm sure you can guess who's on it. The person who has the most to profit if Mr. McGraw should die. The same person who had reason to want to get rid of Marianne McGraw twenty-five years ago."

CULL FELT THE full responsibility of keeping peace at home along with running the ranch, with his father in the hospital. Blake Ryan had handled that job for years. But a couple of years ago he had stepped down, and Cull, as oldest son, had moved into the position alongside his father.

Running the ranch, he could do. It was keeping peace in the house that was the problem. Patricia had been on a rampage since yesterday. He'd heard her yelling at Frieda, their elderly family cook, this morning. He'd broken that up only to find that Nikki St. James had taken off before breakfast and no one knew where she'd gone.

Had she seen how useless this was and left? He could only hope, but even as he thought it, he knew better. Nikki wasn't a quitter. Wherever she'd gone, she'd be back.

As crazy as things had been, he hoped that his father's heart attack would be a wake-up call for him. Something had to change.

"How is he?" Cull asked the nurse when he reached his father's hospital floor after driving in from the ranch.

"He's doing well," she said. "You can see him. Just keep your visit short and don't upset him."

That meant not mentioning Nikki or the twins or Patty or Kitten or the ranch, Cull thought as he walked down the hall. He hesitated at his father's door. He'd watched the man get sicker and sicker and hadn't been able to do anything. Travers McGraw was stubborn; Cull knew that only too well. But maybe now he was ready to face things.

As he walked into the room, he saw that his father's eyes were closed and he was breathing steadily. He stood for a moment, simply relieved. He was glad to see his father's color was better. Stepping to the bed, he touched his hand.

His father's eyes opened and he smiled. "Hope I didn't give you a scare."

Cull chuckled. "Naw, we all just finished our meals before rushing you to the hospital," he joked.

"I'm fine," his father assured him. "The doctor said it was a minor heart attack and he's already lectured me, so you don't have to."

He nodded. Travers McGraw was anything but fine. He needed to make some changes in his life. If he didn't realize that now…

"Is Ms. St. James still at the house?"

Technically, she'd spent last night in the pool house, where Patricia had exiled her, and was gone before he'd gotten up. But he said, "She is," hoping his father would ask him to send her away.

"Good. I still want her to do the book, no matter how it turns out."

He wanted to argue with his father, but he bit his tongue. "Okay."

"I'd appreciate it if you would help her, do whatever she needs."

His father was asking too much, but he nodded, thinking of working closely with Ms. St. James. He had a sudden vision of her swimming half-naked in the pool on a moonlit night— Where had that come from? He smothered the thought, but it took a while for the heat in his belly to go away.

"Is Kitten all right? I hope I didn't scare her."

Cull chuckled at that. "Little scares Kitten."

"So you'll see to it that Ms. St. James gets everything she needs."

He'd love to see to her…needs. "I will."

"Good." His father seemed to relax. He closed his eyes and for a moment, Cull thought he'd dropped back to sleep.

"I can't tell you how much it means to me to have you for a son, Cull." His father opened his eyes again and reached for his hand. "I know I can depend on you and your brothers."

The nurse came in then and shooed Cull out. He promised to come back later and left the hospital.

On the way back to the ranch, he spent most of the time grumbling to himself. By the time he reached the front door of the house, he'd made up his mind.

He would do exactly what his father asked him to do. He'd help Nikki in every way possible. And once she realized there was nothing new to write, she would leave. His father would be disappointed, but he was going to be disappointed anyway.

As he parked in front of the house, he saw that Nikki wasn't back. He wondered where she'd gotten off to so early in the morning and if she'd tell him if he asked. He headed for the pool house only to cross paths with Kitten.

"She's not there," the teen said. "I heard her tell Frieda that she was going into town to do some research." Kitten made it sound like Nikki had lied. "I bet she's meeting a man." Her eyes glinted with mischief. "Which means you got dumped. Looks like you'll never get a girlfriend, even one you had to run over with your truck."

He had wondered how long it would take for that little tidbit to get around. Now he knew. "Kitten, there is a big, black spider on your shoulder."

The girl screamed and began running around swatting at her shoulders.

"Sorry, it wasn't a spider. It was that chip you have on your shoulder."

She mugged a face at him. "I'm going to tell Mother."

"Be my guest." He headed for the stables, wondering what kind of research Nikki was doing in town. Or if Kitten was right and Nikki had lied.

ALL THE WAY back to the ranch, Nikki told herself she'd done the right thing going to the sheriff. If nothing came of it or if she was dead wrong, then at least she'd shared her suspicions.

Now she had to get on with her work. As soon as she reached the ranch, she went looking for Patricia. As a true crime writer, she'd learned that where she found the truth was in the inconsistencies. Not just slight changes in a person's story, but new information that they hadn't remembered before. It always surprised her. Small tidbits were often drawn up from some well of memory to surprise both her and her interviewee.

While she also looked for changes in the stories, she found that those who had the most to hide had almost memorized their statements. They would provide an almost word-for-word account even as many as twenty-five years later.

After something horrible happened, of course people often changed. How much or how little was also often a clue. In Patricia's case, the change had been huge.

Nikki had read Travers's testimony as well as Patricia's from the sheriff's reports along with hundreds of newspaper articles. Travers had awakened to find his wife gone and had rushed out into the hallway on hearing Patty's screams. He raced down the hall to find the window near the twins' cribs wide-open, the cribs empty and a ladder leaning against the side of the house.

He saw no one, but had raced outside only to find footprints in the soft dirt under the window. He'd immediately called the sheriff.

It wasn't until later that he saw Marianne. She'd apparently gone for a swim in the middle of the night because she was coming from the pool house.

Nikki had a pretty good idea that Patty's story would be the same one she had told dozens and dozens of times after the kidnapping. But still she needed to hear it herself.

As she entered the house, she heard voices coming from the kitchen. Patty's voice carried well and while Nikki couldn't make out her words, she could hear the tone. Patty was unhappy with someone.

She found her at the breakfast bar in front of a muffin. From the tension in the room, Patricia had been having a heated discussion with the cook, Frieda Holmes. Clearly Nikki had just interrupted it.

The cook turned her back to the stove, but not before Nikki had seen her blotched red face and her tears.

"I hope this is a good time," she said, knowing full well that it wasn't. What had the two been discussing that had them both so upset? "Mrs. McGraw, I need to ask you some questions."

"You can't be serious," Patricia said, shoving away her crumb-filled plate. "My husband is in the hospital possibly dying and you're intent on—"

"Doing what he asked me to do. I know you

told the authorities what happened that night, but I need to hear it from you. The sooner I get everything I need, the sooner I will be gone."

Patricia sighed. "Not here," she said, glancing at the cook's back. Frieda didn't seem to hear. Or at least didn't react. "Let's go into Travers's office."

Nikki followed her, thinking about yesterday and the first time she'd seen Travers. She was glad to hear he was doing better and would be allowed to have visitors later today.

As if thinking the same thing Nikki was, Patricia said, "When I see my husband this afternoon, I'm going to convince him to put an end to this book of yours."

"You do realize I can write the book without his permission."

Patricia huffed as she sat down at her husband's desk. "Well, I have nothing to add."

Maybe. Maybe not. "I wanted to ask you about Marianne. You were living in the house. You would know if there were problems between her and her husband. If there was another man." She looked down at her notes and turned on her digital recorder. "In other interviews, you've said she'd been acting…strangely."

Clearly Patricia had expected to simply tell the same old story she'd been telling about that night. Her dislike of Marianne became quickly evident. "*Strangely* was putting it mildly. She would wander around the backyard as if lost. I thought for sure she'd lost her mind and as it turns out…"

"What about her relationship with her husband?" Nikki purposely avoided saying Travers's name.

Patricia rolled her eyes and seemed to relax a little. Gossip was clearly something she could get her teeth into. "I knew the minute I was hired that there was trouble in that marriage. I'd seen the signs. It wasn't my first rodeo. Marianne was miserable and not just because of this unexpected pregnancy. That's right, the twins were an accident." She nodded enthusiastically as she leaned closer. "From the start I could tell that she didn't want them."

"Was there another man?"

With a sigh, Patricia sat back. "You should have seen the way she was with that horse trainer. She made a fuss over him. It was so obvious."

"I'm sure her husband must have noticed."

Patricia shook her head in disgust. "He was blind to anything she did. Sure he noticed, but he thought she was just being nice to him since he was away from his wife and child and clearly lonely."

"Maybe that's all it was."

"Then why would the two of them cook up this kidnapping scheme?" Patricia demanded.

"Maybe they didn't. When the horse trainer was arrested, he didn't have the money. Neither did Marianne. So what happened to the ransom money?"

Patricia shrugged. "Maybe he hid it, waiting until the two of them could run away together."

"Strange, though, that it hasn't been found. I know the authorities searched the ranch for any sign of the money—and the twins."

"You mean searched for graves."

"But they found nothing."

"Have you taken a look at this country around the ranch? It's Missouri Breaks, miles and miles of nothing but gullies and cliffs and pines, millions of places to hide anything you want."

Nikki couldn't argue that. "Let's talk about that night."

Patricia proceeded to tell her story almost verbatim from her other accounts. Just as Nikki had assumed, she got the same old, same old.

Patricia claimed she'd been awakened by a noise and gotten up to check the twins. As she'd crossed the hall, she'd been surprised to feel the breeze coming in—convinced she'd left their window closed.

On entering the room, she'd gone to close it

when she noticed that one of the cribs was empty. She'd quickly checked the other and panicked.

"I stepped to the window, saw the ladder and the footprints below and started screaming."

"Tell me where everyone else was at that point."

She frowned. "It's really a blur. Everyone came running down the hallway toward the nursery. Travers got there first and then the kids. Travers told me to take the children to my room and stay there to wait for the sheriff. That's about the time Marianne showed up, her hair wet. I didn't realize until later that she'd been for a swim—in the middle of the night." She rolled her eyes, making it clear she thought the woman had been crazy even back then.

"Let's not forget that Jesse Rose's blanket was found in the pool house after the kidnapping," Patricia said and raised an eyebrow.

Jesse Rose's blanket. So that's what the kidnapper had left behind? She tried not to give away her surprise in her expression. "And you had all three boys with you?"

The woman started to nod, but stopped. "No, Ledger was always the one lagging behind. I saw him down the hall and called to him."

"Had he come from his room?"

"No." She frowned, seeming surprised by her answer. "His bare feet were all muddy. I had to wash them in my tub in my room before I let him get into my bed. But that was nothing unusual. Ledger often went out at night and wandered around. Like Marianne."

"Did he say anything to you that night about where he'd been or what he might have seen?"

"Seen?" She scoffed at the idea. "He was a child. Three years old. Cull was only seven and Boone, he was barely five. None of them said a word. I put them all into my bed. Like me, they were wide-eyed with terror and listening to what was going on outside my room."

AFTER TALKING TO PATTY, Nikki went looking for Ledger. But when she reached the barn, it was Cull who she found feeding the horses.

"Have you seen Ledger?" she asked.

"He's gone into town for breakfast," Cull said without looking at her.

Abby, she thought, and her heart went out to him.

"Well, since I have you…" she said.

He stopped what he was doing to give her his full attention. "So you think you have me, huh? You think you have the entire family now." He shook his head.

She ignored him. Patricia had proven Nikki's theory this morning. There'd been a slight change in her story, giving Nikki new information that Patricia hadn't remembered before. It was something small, something that even Nikki wasn't sure mattered.

"What part of 'it's not safe for you to be here' don't you get?" he demanded.

"I've been around horses before—just not unbroken stallions let out into a corral I happen to be in."

He ignored the accusation. "Not *here* in the stables. On this ranch. Didn't dinner last night teach you anything?"

"The soup *wasn't* poisoned," she said as she stepped closer to rub a horse's neck.

"The point is in this house it could have been," he said without looking at her. "You have no idea. The past twenty-five years…" He shook his head as if he couldn't go on. "Everyone is sick of hearing about the kidnapping let alone talking about it."

"Everyone but your father."

A muscle in his jaw jumped. "My father is the kind of man who just doesn't give up."

"What kind of man are you?"

He shifted those blue eyes to her, welding her to the spot. "The kind who knows a lost cause when he sees one."

"We've already had this argument. I'm not leaving and I'm guessing your father isn't giving up. He still wants me to do the book." She narrowed her eyes at him. "And unless I'm wrong, which I don't believe I am, he asked you to help me."

He chuckled as he shook his head again. "All you're doing is making things worse for everyone, including yourself."

"Don't you want to know the kind of woman I am?" When he said nothing, she continued. "I'm like your father. When I start something I finish it."

Cull seemed to consider that before he turned toward her, his lips quirking into a grin as his eyes blazed with challenge. "Is that right?"

Before she could react, he grabbed her and dragged her to him. His mouth dropped to hers in a demanding kiss as he pushed her back against the barn wall.

Fleetingly she wondered how far he would go. He was angry, frustrated with what was happening to his family, scared. She knew those emotions only too well.

But she thought she also knew Cull McGraw. No matter what her grandfather said, she thought she was a pretty good judge of character. Cull wasn't the kind of man who would force a woman. He didn't have to. He was trying to scare her—just as he had with his talk of evil here on the ranch.

She did her best not to react to the kiss. It was a fine one even though she hadn't asked for it and his heart wasn't really in it. But she'd felt his fire, his passion fueled by the well of emotions surging through him.

The kiss made her want a real one from him, which was more dangerous for her than a wild stallion. The kiss ended as abruptly as it had started. Cull shoved off the barn wall and took two steps back. If anything, he looked more upset than he had before.

"You should be afraid of me," he said, his voice rough with emotion as he jerked off his straw cowboy hat and raked a hand through his thick dark hair. "I even scare myself."

"You don't scare me."

"Then you are more foolish than I thought. What happened here changed us all. If you can't feel the malice…" His gaze shifted toward the open barn door. She could see the house in the distance.

Nikki looked toward the nursery window. The curtain moved but it could have merely been the breeze stirring it.

When she looked at Cull again, all she saw was his backside headed out to pasture. She watched him go, aware of the lingering taste and scent of him, both more disturbing than she'd wanted to admit earlier.

Now she found herself alone in the barn where her father had worked all those years ago. An eerie quiet seemed to fall over it in Cull's absence.

She moved to the horse she'd petted earlier and again rubbed its neck, needing to feel the warmth. Cull was right. She could feel malice here, but unlike him, she didn't believe in dark spirits.

Instead, she believed that evil lived in the heart of man—and woman. She thought of Sheriff McCall Crawford and wondered if she'd do anything about her suspicions. Nikki was anxious to find out if she'd been right, if her instincts hadn't let her down.

Meanwhile, those instincts told her that someone in this house knew what had happened to the twins. She'd never felt it more strongly.

A breeze rustled the nearby pines, making the boughs groan softly. A hinge creaked somewhere deep in the barn. The hair quilled on the back of her neck, a gust of cold air rushing over her skin to raise goose bumps.

Suddenly she had the feeling she was no longer alone. She shuddered at what felt like breath on the back of her neck. As she rushed toward the barn door, she told herself she didn't believe in evil ghosts. Whatever she'd just felt in the barn was only her overactive imagination, nothing more.

And yet the feeling hung with her all the way to the pool house.

Chapter Twelve

Nikki closed the pool house door behind her, shaken by whatever that had been in the barn. She told herself it was a reaction to Cull. Every run-in with him left her off-kilter. He was angry and afraid—she could understand that. But kissing her? That had scared him more than it had her.

At least that's what she thought. He wanted her gone. Well, it couldn't be soon enough for Nikki, she thought, surprised she felt that way. She wasn't safe here from herself. She didn't scare easily, but Cull was right. There was something on the wind that turned her blood to ice.

Not that she could leave before she was done. Which reminded her that she needed to take advantage of whatever time she had here. She glanced through the window toward the house. Earlier she'd heard just enough of what Patricia had been saying to the cook this morning, to make her anxious to talk to Frieda.

At the main house, Nikki entered the kitchen to find Frieda Holmes sitting in a chair in the corner. The cook had a threaded needle in her hand and a quilt lay over her lap. Nikki had seen her elderly neighbor sew on a quilt binding enough times that she knew at once what the woman was doing.

"What a beautiful quilt," she said. "Did you sew it yourself?"

Frieda nodded almost shyly. She was a small, almost homely woman with dark hair shot with gray. She was in her early sixties, by Nikki's calculations, and had been the cook for years. That was back before they could afford a full-time nanny. Back before the twins.

Nikki moved closer. "I love the colors, and your quilting is amazing. My goodness, it's all done by hand." This surprised her, since her neighbor quilted with a sewing machine and only hand sewed the binding.

"It relaxes me," Frieda said proudly as she ran a hand over the tiny, closely spaced stitches.

At the sound of footfalls behind her, Nikki turned as Patricia came into the kitchen. "What's going on?" she demanded.

Frieda stuck her finger with the needle as she hurriedly tried to put the quilt away. She tucked the needle in the fabric and shoved the quilt into a bag next to the chair. She wiped the blood from her stuck finger on a corner of her apron and rushed to her feet.

"I was waiting on the pies in the oven," the cook said as if feeling guilty for getting off her feet for even a break.

"And I was just admiring Frieda's quilt," Nikki said.

Patricia dismissed that with a flip of her hand. "I've never understood why anyone would want to cut up perfectly good fabric and then sew it back together. It makes no sense."

"It makes beautiful quilts," Nikki said, seeing how Patricia's remark had hurt Frieda's feelings. "My neighbor quilts. Unfortunately, I've never taken the time to learn."

"Well, if you like quilts that much, you should drive out to Old Town and visit the Whitehorse Sewing Circle." Patricia turned to Frieda. "Don't you still meet in the community center down there? It's not that far from here. There are always a bunch of old ladies in the back working on a quilt. Isn't that right, Frieda?"

Frieda looked even more upset. Was it the crack about old ladies? Or something else? "I would love to do that," Nikki said. "Is there a certain day I could go?"

But it was her boss who answered for the

cook. "Frieda goes on her day off, Wednesday. I'm sure she'd be happy to take you." There was something in Patricia's tone, an underlying menace, that made no sense to Nikki.

The timer on the oven went off and Frieda quickly picked up two hot pads and opened the oven without saying a word.

"I'm going into town to the hospital to see my husband," Patricia announced as she looked at Nikki. "You might not be here by Wednesday if Travers has decided to stop this ridiculous book." She waved a hand through the air, not giving Nikki a chance to remind the woman that she could do the book without Travers's permission, before she turned to Frieda.

"There are fresh vegetables from the garden that need to be washed and refrigerated right away," the woman said to the cook. "Please don't keep Frieda from her work," she said to Nikki. "I believe Cull has a horse saddled and waiting for you. He told me to tell you to have Frieda provide you with a picnic lunch. Apparently, he's taking you for a horseback ride." Her gaze took in what Nikki was wearing. "You might want to change."

With that she spun on her heel and stormed out in a cloud of expensive perfume.

Cull was taking her on a horseback ride? That was news to her. Frieda still seemed upset even with Patricia gone as she took out four beautiful apple pies from the oven. Nikki noticed that the woman's hands were shaking. Patricia had upset her and it was unclear to Nikki how exactly other than the woman's demanding and demeaning tone. So why was Frieda still working for her? Surely she could get a job elsewhere.

"I'll put together a picnic lunch for you while you change," the cook said, clearly wanting Nikki out of her kitchen.

"Thank you." She left to go change and when she returned, Frieda handed her an insulated bag heavy with food. As she thanked her again, Frieda busied herself washing the vegetables as per her boss's orders.

On the way to the barn, Nikki wondered if this horseback picnic ride was Cull's idea—or Patricia's. Either way, it would give her time alone with him away from a lot of the drama.

CULL WATCHED THROUGH the open doorway as Nikki made her way down to the barn. She'd changed from the slacks, blouse and high heels she'd been wearing earlier. Now she was in a pair of jeans, a T-shirt and tennis shoes. He should have realized she wouldn't own any cowboy boots.

Still, she looked good. She had a bag in one hand, no doubt their picnic lunch. He smiled to himself. The horseback ride had been Patricia's idea when she'd found him in the barn.

"Get her out of here for a while," the woman had said, and he hadn't needed to ask whom she was referring to. "Take her for a horseback ride. Even better, leave her out there in the wilds. Or…" A look had come over his stepmother. "Or cut her cinch so she has an accident. Just joking," she added quickly at his mock shocked expression.

Patricia had caught him at just the right time. He felt antsy and knew exactly what he needed, and it was to get on the back of a horse and ride out of here. "I'll take her for a ride," he said, making Patricia smile.

As Nikki approached the barn, he said, "I should have asked you if you rode."

"Or if I wanted to go on a picnic with you," she said but was smiling. "I have ridden before. Once at a fair when I was a child."

Great, he thought. Green. Just what he needed. "I have a mild-mannered horse you'll like." He could see that she was trying to think of a good reason to say no. Who could blame her after earlier in the barn? That had been stupid kissing her. What had he been thinking?

And then springing this horseback ride and picnic on her. If he was her, he'd be suspicious.

"You should see the ranch," he said, determined that she would go with him. "Consider it research. Also I know you're dying to get me alone so you can…grill me."

She was looking skeptically at the horse he'd saddled for her. "I'm not sure about this." It had been too long since she'd been on the back of a horse, but he didn't like leaving her here alone with almost everyone gone.

"Where is that woman who will stop at nothing to get what she wants?" he asked her.

She smiled and looked resigned.

"Hey, it's going to be fun. Trust me. You're in good hands with me."

Clearly, she wasn't so sure about that. But he'd promised his father he would help her. And wasn't that what he was doing? But how long before she realized there was nothing new to write about? How long before she realized that she'd wasted her time coming here?

Soon, he hoped. She didn't want to believe it, but she'd put herself in danger. She had a reputation for getting to the truth. What if there was someone on the ranch who had more to hide than he did?

He hadn't been trying to scare her. There was something evil in that house. He'd felt it too many times. But unlike Nikki, he couldn't leave here. His father needed him. So did his mother.

He thought of Marianne. He needed to go

visit her and tell her about his father's heart attack. Not that she might hear him, let alone understand. But he felt he owed her that. She had the right to know. He often told her about things going on at the ranch.

She would rock, holding those horrible dolls, and he would tell her about the horses they'd bought and sold. His mother had always loved horses, loved to ride. It was something she had shared with her husband. Unlike Patricia, who didn't ride and complained that horses smelled. Kitten was just as bad. Which was fine with Cull. It meant that they never came down to the barns.

Cull shoved away any thoughts of Patricia as he led the horses out of the barn. Soon he and Nikki would be lost in the wilds of the Missouri Breaks. Just the thought stirred an unexpected desire. Nikki St. James was more dangerous than she realized.

Fortunately she wouldn't be with them long.

Chapter Thirteen

Nikki's mind was still racing with what had happened in the kitchen. The relationship between Frieda and Patricia perplexed her. Why wouldn't Patricia want her talking to Frieda? What was she worried the cook would tell her? And yet she'd suggested Frieda take her to her quilt group?

Just her showing up at a crime scene like this was often a catalyst that brought secrets to the surface. Nikki thought of the other books she'd researched and the times she'd uncovered so much that it had almost cost her her life. While that should have been a warning, she knew she had to get Frieda alone so she'd have a chance to talk to her without Patricia being around.

But right now she had something more troublesome to occupy her thoughts. Getting on a horse and riding off into the wilds with Cull. He took the picnic lunch, stuffed it into a saddlebag on his horse, then grabbed a straw cowboy hat hanging on the wall and dropped it on her head.

"You'll be glad you have it, trust me," he said as he cupped his hands to hoist her up into the saddle. She hadn't been completely truthful about her experience with horses. Her mother had been deathly afraid of them and had passed that fear on to her. Which was strange, since Nikki's father had trained horses.

Sitting high in the saddle, she watched Cull swing gracefully up onto his horse. He gave it a nudge with his boot heels and started out of the corral. For a moment, she thought her horse wasn't going to move. She gave it a nudge with the heels of her tennis shoes. Nothing. Cull looked back over his shoulder at her. Grinning, he let out a whistle and her horse began to follow him.

Nikki clung to the saddlehorn, feeling as if she might fall off the horse at any moment.

"You'll get use to the rhythm," Cull said, still grinning as her horse trotted up next to his. "Just relax."

"Easy for you to say. You've probably been riding since you were born."

"Not quite. I must have been close to a year old the first time."

They rode out of the corral, past the stand of trees behind the house and into the pasture.

Ahead, the land opened into rolling prairie that stretched to the Little Rockies. She could see steep cliffs of rock shining in the sunshine and huge stands of pines.

"You're doing fine," Cull said, his voice gentle. She looked over at him and tried to relax. She had a stray thought. Cull was the kind of man a woman could fall hard for. She watched him run one of his big, sun-browned hands over his horse's neck, an affectionate caress. She imagined his hand touching her like that and had to look away.

"It's beautiful out here," she said. The afternoon light had an intensity that made the landscape glow. She sat up in the saddle a little straighter, feeling a little more confident. The horse hadn't taken off at a dead run, hadn't bucked, hadn't lain down and tried to roll over, hadn't ditched her the first chance it got.

All in all, she thought things were going pretty well—if she didn't think about the fact that soon she would be entirely alone with the man next to her. The same one she'd heard say he would "take care" of her.

CULL FELT AT home in the saddle. He felt the strain of the last twenty-four hours drain from him as they rode toward the Missouri Breaks. What he loved most about this country was the wild openness and the lack of people. He'd read that the population was only .03 persons per square mile out here. He didn't need anyone to tell him that there were more cattle than humans.

He glanced over at Nikki. She seemed comfortable in the saddle. He'd chosen a gentle horse for her, one of his favorites. His gaze shifted to the country ahead of them. It dropped toward the Missouri River in rolling prairie, becoming wilder with each mile as they skirted the Little Rockies.

They didn't talk as they rode, the sun lounging overhead in a brilliant blue sky filled with cumulous clouds. A faint breeze bent the deep grasses and kept the day cool.

"What an amazing day," Nikki said when they stopped near an outcropping of rocks in a stand of pine trees. There was plenty of shade, so Cull thought they could have some lunch here.

They hadn't talked on the ride. He had gotten the impression that like him Nikki was enjoying the peace and quiet, something sorely missing on the ranch. But he was smart enough to know it was temporary. He hadn't forgotten why she was here.

He watched her push back the straw cowboy hat and squint at him. Even though he knew what was coming, he didn't care. The warm afternoon sun glowed on her face. She really was stunning in a not-so-classical way.

Sure she was attractive, but he liked to think he wasn't the kind of man who could be taken in by looks alone. A part of him admired the hell out of her. The woman had fortitude—that was for sure. He thought of all the journalists who had tried to get stories over the years. Where they'd failed to get a foot in the door, Nikki St. James had the run of the house—and the ranch.

They ate, both seemingly lost in their own thoughts. He was curious about her childhood, but didn't want to break the peaceful quiet between them to ask.

As he was putting away the last of the picnic, she finally brought up the kidnapping. He'd been waiting, knowing she couldn't possibly not take advantage of the two of them being alone.

"I need to ask you about that night and even the days leading up to it," she said almost apologetically. "I'd rather do it out here than back at the house, if you don't mind."

To his surprise, he realized he didn't. His father had asked him to cooperate, so he would. He'd rather get it over with out here than back at the ranch anyway. He lay back against one of the smooth rocks and looked out toward the Breaks, dark with pine trees and deep gullies.

"You were seven," she continued. "I'm guessing the sheriff and FBI didn't question you at any length."

He shook his head. "Because I didn't know anything."

NIKKI HAD HOPED after the horseback ride that Cull would be more forthcoming. She wasn't going to let him put her off. She moved so she could look into his blue eyes, determined to find out what he was hiding.

"You've had years to think about that night. I think you know more than you've ever told anyone. I think you're protecting someone. Your mother?"

Cull looked away for a moment. "My mother had nothing to do with this."

"You know why the sheriff and the FBI believe it was an inside job and that your mother might have been involved," she said carefully. "A bottle of codeine cough syrup that had been prescribed to your mother was found in the twins' room. That's why they speculated that the twins had been drugged to keep them quiet during the kidnapping."

"It wasn't my mother," Cull said with more force than he'd obviously intended as he turned back to her.

Nikki heard something in his voice. Fear.

"The cough syrup wasn't just her prescription. Her fingerprints were the only ones on the bottle, but," she said quickly before he could argue, "maybe the twins weren't drugged with the cough syrup. Maybe it was left there to frame your mother."

He stared at her for a long moment. "Why are you giving her the benefit of doubt?"

"Because I've often found that things aren't what they seem. If I'm good at anything, it's realizing that."

She saw him waver. "Still, there had to be someone inside the house who had access to the cough syrup and helped get the twins out of their cribs and to the window and the person on the ladder," he said.

"Patricia had access to the cough syrup. Maybe she'd given one of you older kids some. Do you remember having a cold or cough?"

He shook his head. "Are you saying Patty—"

"Not necessarily. That wing is isolated from the rest of the house and has an entrance and exit just down the stairs from the twins' room— anyone could have been let in. Someone inside the house could have taken the cough syrup before the kidnapping to frame her."

"Exactly. Which brings us back to the same spot. Someone in the house was in on it. Someone let the kidnapper in. Someone got hold of my mother's cough syrup."

"Which is why I need to know what you remember."

"I told you—"

"I know you're holding something back, Cull."

He sat up and for a moment she thought he might get up to leave. But instead, he settled again, then snapped, "You're a mind reader now?"

"No, I just know that often when people are afraid, it's because they know something that they fear will hurt someone they love. You and your mother were close, weren't you?" Cull still visited his mother. She knew that from her visit with Tess at the mental hospital. "Isn't it time that you told someone what you saw that night?"

He looked away. A muscle jumped along his strong jawline.

"What is it that you're so terrified I'm going to find out?" Nikki demanded.

Cull didn't move. "Why did you have to come here?"

She heard such anguish in his voice that it broke her heart, but she said nothing, waiting.

"I saw my mother."

Relief flooded her. "That night?"

He nodded as he returned his gaze to her.

He looked resigned and she wondered if a huge weight hadn't come off his shoulders. She knew only too well what secrets could do to a person.

"It was earlier that I saw her. She'd just come out of the twins' room," he said as if seeing it all again. "She looked right through me. It was as if she didn't see me until I spoke."

"Is it possible she was sleepwalking?"

He seemed surprised by the question. "She did walk in her sleep and had since she was a child, which according to the doctor implied a neurological problem that had gone undiagnosed. But to me, she seemed completely out of it. Now I wonder if she wasn't in shock."

"You think she'd already been to the nursery and found the twins missing?"

"I don't know." Cull shook his head before leaning back against the rocks where they were sitting. "I saw her walk down the hallway. I followed her, afraid she might hurt herself. I didn't think to check on the twins."

She heard the naked guilt strain his voice. "You were a child. It wasn't your place—"

As if he'd said all this to himself already and not believed it, he said, "If my mother was in on the kidnapping, then maybe the twins were already gone. Or maybe that's when she gave the twins the cough syrup. It wasn't much later that the twins were found missing. If I had told someone, they might have caught the kidnapper before he could get away with them."

Nikki considered that for a few moments, her heart aching at the guilt she saw in his face. "You said you followed your mother that night?"

"She must have heard me behind her, because she stopped and told me to go back to bed. That everything was going to be all right. She said she was going for a swim." His blue eyes shone with unshed tears. "Do you see why I have kept that to myself all these years? It only makes her look more guilty since we know the kidnapper was in the pool house that night after the twins were taken."

She knew that the FBI agents were convinced that Marianne had met her co-kidnapper in the pool house that night and that the swim had just been a ruse.

Nikki gave him a few moments before she asked, "What were you doing in the hallway that night?"

He frowned as if he'd never asked himself that question. "I was looking for Ledger. When I woke I looked into this room and saw that he wasn't in his bed. He had a habit of wandering around the ranch at night. I had gone looking for him."

"Did you go outside?"

He shook his head. "That's when I heard Patty

screaming. She was standing outside the twins' room screaming that they were gone. My first thought was that my mother had taken them somewhere, which was terrifying enough given the way she was acting. The way she had been acting since their births."

"It was speculated that she was suffering from postpartum depression."

He nodded. "She kept saying she was fine but something was definitely wrong. She seemed confused a lot of the time and complained of not feeling well, but when my father took her to the doctor, he couldn't find anything wrong with her."

Nikki knew that he'd just described his father's recent condition. They'd all just assumed it was over the anniversary of the kidnapping just as they'd assumed Marianne's was postpartum depression.

"Did you see anyone else in the hallway that night?" Nikki asked.

"Everyone came out of their rooms after they heard Patty screaming and ran down to the nursery. I just remember Dad going past."

She stared at him. "But you didn't go." She saw it on his handsome face, the anguish, the fear, the regret.

He shook his head. "Somehow, I knew the twins were gone and something horrible had happened. I was terrified that my mother had done something to them."

"What about your brothers Ledger and Boone? When did you see them?"

Cull frowned again as if picturing it in his mind. "Boone came out of his room, but I don't remember seeing Ledger until later."

From what Patty had told her, there was a good chance that Ledger had been out roaming the ranch that night. Three was old enough to remember in some instances. Nikki herself could remember things that had happened at that age. Maybe Ledger remembered something. But hadn't been old enough to realize that what he'd seen at the time had been the kidnapper.

"Enjoy your ride?" Patricia demanded when Cull came into the house, Nikki at his side. "Your father is being released from the ho· pital. Ledger and Boone have gone in to pick him up. I wanted to go, but you know how they can be."

The woman picked nervously at the suit jacket she was wearing. "I want everything to be perfect when he gets here." Her gaze shifted to Nikki. "I think it would be better if she wasn't here."

"Patricia—"

"I don't care what your father wants at this

point. He could have died. All this is too upsetting for him. He needs his rest."

Cull shook his head. "I talked to the doctor this morning. Dad is doing well. In fact, his health has improved since he's been in the hospital or the doctor wouldn't be releasing him."

"I just don't want him upset," she said, holding her ground.

"Well, sending Nikki away would upset him, since he was very specific about that."

The woman let out a sigh. "Fine, but if she kills him, don't blame me." With that, she turned and stormed off toward the kitchen.

Cull cursed under his breath. "That woman is going to be the death of all of us."

Nikki watched her go, thinking again of the symptoms that both Marianne and Travers shared—although twenty-five years apart. The common denominator was that both had been living in this house at the time.

Well, she'd done what she could by going to the sheriff. Now it was in McCall Crawford's hands.

"I think I'm going to go rest for a while," she said, looking at the time.

Cull nodded as if he thought it was a good idea for her to be away when his father arrived back at the house.

The horseback ride had been wonderful, but

she felt sunburned and tired. While glad Travers was being released, she worried about what he was coming home to, given her suspicions.

Surely, if she was right, no one would try to harm him now. Nikki had been afraid that Travers would change his mind about letting her stay here for the book. Fortunately he apparently hadn't. She couldn't help feeling bad for him. When she'd seen him collapse, it brought home just how serious this was. She didn't want to inflict any more pain on this family than it had already been through.

She'd seen Cull's pain earlier when he'd told her what he'd seen that night. Like what Patricia had remembered and told her, it was another piece of the intricate puzzle. There were still so many pieces missing, though. Worse, she hated what the final picture would reveal. Maybe her grandfather was right and she was too emotionally involved in this one.

She walked toward the pool house. The wind had come up. It whipped the branches of the cottonwood trees, lashing the new green leaves against the glass. Past the trees, she saw the horses running, their manes and tails blowing back as they cavorted in the deep green of the pasture. She thought about Cull and his brothers and their obvious love for the horses they raised.

The reminder of Cull's hand gently stroking the mare's neck sent a shiver through her.

Nikki told herself that her reaction to Cull was normal. She hadn't met anyone like him and was now thrown together with him in a household where she had few to no allies. What worried her was that the man seemed able to see into her soul. That made him more than a little dangerous. Not to mention he already suspected that her motives for being here had to do with more than just the book. What was he going do when he found out that Nate Corwin was her father?

As she entered the pool house, she walked directly to her bedroom. She would have a shower before dinner, but right now, she just wanted to lie down for a while.

At a sound behind her, she turned to look back into the living room. Had someone been there? A movement near the door caught her eye. She stared as a single sheet of paper slid under the door and was caught by the wind from the window. The paper whirled up off the floor.

Hurriedly stepping to it, Nikki chased the sheet of paper down until she could catch it, then rushed to look out to see who had shoved it under her door.

She saw no one. Wind shook the nearby trees, sending dust and dirt into the air. She cupped a hand over her eyes as she looked in the direction of the house. The curtain moved on the second-floor window of the nursery and then fell silent.

With a shiver, she turned back inside, closing and locking the door behind her before she looked at what she held in her hand.

With a start she saw what appeared to be a page torn from a diary.

Chapter Fourteen

Nikki leaned against the pool house door, her heart pounding as she looked at the sheet of paper in her hand. It appeared to have been torn from a diary or journal, but there were no dates on the page. She began to read it as she walked over to the window, closed it and dropped into a chair.

I heard the screaming last night. Travers said it was just the wind, but I've never heard wind like that ever.

I got up and went up to check the children. I hate having them on a separate floor even knowing that the nanny is close by. But Travers insisted that we move to the lower floor master bedroom as soon as it was finished. He says I need my rest. I feel like all I do it rest. Sometimes I feel like I am going crazy.

In the nursery, the twins looked like sleeping angels. I call them the twins because their names seem too large for such small babies. They scare me they are so small, so fragile.

Just looking at them makes me cry. I feel such anguish, such guilt. When I found out I was pregnant with them, I was upset. I didn't want them. Still don't feel a connection to them. I want to love them, but they are so needy, so demanding. Even when I help Patty with them, I don't feel like I'm their mother. I can tell that she knows, that she's judging me and finding me wanting. I asked Travers to fire her and let me take care of them, but he refused. I'm sure Patty heard us arguing about it.

As I started to leave the twins' room, I saw the light in the stables. I thought about waking Travers, but I have awakened him too many times terrified only to be told there is nothing out in the darkness. Nothing that wants to hurt me, let alone destroy me. So why do I feel this way?

I know I shouldn't go out there alone, but I won't be able to sleep until I know that the horses are all right. That there is nothing out there to fear. Maybe it is only Nate working late. He is such a kind, caring man.

I can talk to him. He seems to understand. He doesn't judge me. He lets me cry without looking at me as if I'm crazy. I'll go for a swim after I check the stables. That seems to help me sleep.

On the back, the text continued.

The light was on again tonight. I am trying to ignore it. Just as I am trying to sleep after my swim. But I'm restless. I know I should stay in the house and not go out there. But I need to see Nate. He is the only—

The words ended abruptly. Nikki turned the page over, forgetting that it was only one diary page. So where was the rest? Her heart was in her throat at the mention of her father. Was this how it had started? Marianne afraid at night and going out to the barn to talk to Nate. *He is such a kind, caring man.* Her father. What had this kind, caring man done to help Marianne McGraw?

She stared at the paper. Who had left this and why? Had they wanted her to believe that her father and Marianne had been lovers? Had the two of them made a plan to get rid of the twins—and have enough money to run away?

More to the point, why had she never heard

that Marianne kept a diary? Who had known about it? Not the FBI or sheriff, or Nikki would have found the information during her research. The diary would also have been mentioned in the court transcripts—even if the judge had excluded it.

And where was the rest of it? Clearly someone on this ranch had the diary.

But why hadn't they turned it over to the FBI at the time of the kidnapping? Because it incriminated Marianne? Or incriminated the person who now had it in their possession?

They wanted her to believe Marianne and Nate had been lovers, had been the kidnappers. But in their attempt to convince her, they'd now made her aware of the diary.

Instead of convincing her, they'd only managed to make her more convinced her father was innocent on all counts.

So who had put it under her door?

NIKKI FOUND CULL in the pasture inspecting one of the horses' hooves.

"Your mother kept a diary?" Nikki demanded.

He looked up in surprise. "I beg your pardon?"

"Why is it that this is the first time I've heard that your mother kept a diary?"

Cull rose slowly to his feet, stretching out

his long legs and then his back, before he said, "Because I didn't know she did—if she did."

Cull and his mother had been close, but it was clear he hadn't known. He looked as surprised as she'd been. "Well, someone knew she did," she said, waving the page she held in her hand.

He caught her wrist with warm strong fingers and slowly pried her fingers open to take the sheet from her.

"Is that your mother's handwriting?" she asked, half afraid he would say it wasn't and that someone was playing an elaborate joke on her.

"It looks like her handwriting." Stepping out of the horse's shadow, he held the page up to the waning sunlight. "Where did you get this?" he demanded after reading it.

"Someone slipped it under my door."

He looked angry as if he wanted to crush it in his big hand, but she snatched it from him before he could. "Whoever gave you that wants you to think my mother had an affair with the horse trainer."

"If true, then why not produce the entire diary?" She shook her head. "Whoever put this under my door wants me to believe that. But if this is the most incriminating part, it doesn't prove your mother had an affair." Nikki prayed she was right. If her father hadn't fallen in love with Marianne, then he had no motive for being involved in the kidnapping.

Cull pulled off his Stetson and raked his fingers through his thick dark hair. "I can't imagine who would have known about the diary."

"And kept it from the FBI and sheriff all these years."

He nodded, frowning.

"You must have seen her with Nate," she said quietly, hating that she couldn't let the subject go.

"No more than I saw her with anyone else. Nate was a nice guy. He gave me a pocket knife and taught me how to whittle so I didn't cut myself."

"You don't think he was involved in the kidnapping."

Cull looked away for a moment before he shrugged. "How well do we really know another person?" His gaze locked with hers just long enough for her to wonder if he knew the truth about her.

His mother had kept a diary. Cull hated to think what might be in the rest of it. Something even more incriminating in the rest? If so, then why did whoever had it wait so long to share even this much of it?

Nikki didn't think whatever was in there

would be more incriminating. He hoped she was right. For years he'd believed in his mother's innocence. The last thing he wanted was to know that he'd been wrong.

But who in this house had it?

There were times he'd certainly wanted to be anyone but a McGraw. All the media attention had been horrible over the years, not to mention the suspicion that had fallen on every member of the household.

Nikki seemed surprised when he showed up at the pool house door, insisting that she come to dinner that night. "Wouldn't it be better if it was just family?"

"Probably, but Patricia invited my father's attorney and friend Blake. I'm sure she thinks they can convince him what a mistake it is having you here."

"I would think everyone would be happy if I was gone, you included," she said.

He met her gaze. "Don't presume to know how I feel."

She looked at him as if surprised by that. "So you don't want to get rid of me?"

"Maybe I just want to see an end to this. My father promised that if nothing comes of your... book, then he will quit searching for the twins."

So that was it. "Is there a reason the attorney and former ranch manager wouldn't want the truth about the kidnapping to come out?" she asked, recalling what he said about Patricia using them at dinner tonight.

"They're both protective of my father—and Patty, for that matter. Blake knows my father will always take care of him because of the years he put in here. As for the family attorney, Jim Waters is pretty happy the way things are now with my father continuing to pay him to look into claims by those believing they either know something about the kidnapping or are one of the twins. If Jim didn't have a gambling problem, he'd be quite wealthy by now."

"So if I find out what really happened to the twins, it will put Waters out of business?"

Cull smiled. "Not completely, but it would hurt because he would have to go back to just being the family lawyer. We should get on up to the house. You're sure you're up to this?"

She was sore from her horseback ride and it was clear that he knew it. "I'm fine."

He smiled. "Yes, you are."

Everyone had already gathered outside the dining room when she and Cull came in from outside.

Travers McGraw saw her from his wheelchair and turned toward her, extending his hand. She took it in both of hers. "The wheelchair was doctor's orders. He wants me to rest, but I assure you I'm fine. Better than ever."

He did look better, she admitted. "I'm so glad. I was worried."

"No need. I'm just glad you're still here. Are you making progress?"

Before she could answer, Patricia interrupted to say that dinner was served. They filed into the dining room, Travers insisting they all go ahead of him. All Nikki could think about was the last time they were all in here.

A hush fell over the group after they were all seated at their places. Patricia stood and clinked her butter knife against her empty wineglass. "I just want to say how happy I am to have my husband home." She beamed down the table at him. "I'm glad you are all here to celebrate." Her gaze lit on Nikki, but quickly moved to attorney Jim Waters. She gave him a meaningful look before she sat down and Frieda began to pour the wine.

Nikki noticed that everyone but Travers was subdued. She could feel the tension. This was not a welcome-home celebration. It was exactly what Cull had suspected—a bushwhacking. Patricia wanted the lawyer and former ranch manager to talk Travers into forgetting about the kidnapping book.

She noticed that even Kitten wasn't her usual

self. She fidgeted until the first course was brought out and then barely touched her food.

It wasn't until right before dessert that Jim Waters cleared his voice and said, "Travers, we're all glad you're all right. But I think we need to talk about the future."

Travers cut him off at once. "If this is about the book Nikki is researching here, please save your breath, Jim. I hope my heart attack will only make her that much more determined to find out the truth about that night."

Nikki smiled at him.

"I think you should hear them out," Patricia said, and smiled sweetly.

"We know what this means to you," Waters continued. "But at what cost? You have three sons, a wife and a stepdaughter to think about. If you were to—"

"I'm sorry, Jim, but I've made myself perfectly clear on this," Travers said, putting down his fork. "I won't hear any more about this subject from any of you." He looked pointedly at his wife.

"Then you need to know who this woman really is," Waters said, getting to his feet to point an accusing finger at Nikki.

She felt her heart drop as she saw the satisfaction in his gaze. He knew and now he was about to destroy her credibility with Travers and there was nothing she could do about it.

"She isn't here just to write a book about the kidnapping. She's—"

"We already know," Cull said, cutting Waters off.

"You *don't* know." Jim Waters looked furious that he'd been interrupted. "Nate Corwin—"

"Was her father," Cull said, finishing his sentence.

"What?" Patricia demanded, and looked to her husband as if this was the first time she was hearing about it. No one at the table bought her act.

All the air rushed out of the attorney in a gush as he looked at Travers for confirmation. He'd been so sure he was about to drop a bombshell.

Nikki couldn't breathe. Her gaze was on Cull. How long had he known? She looked toward Travers. Did he know?

"Your *father* was Nate Corwin, the man who…?" Patricia acted as if it was so horrible she couldn't even finish.

Travers smiled at Nikki and reached over to pat her hand. "Cull told me everything."

"Well, it would have been nice if someone had bothered to tell me," Patricia said, her face flushed with anger. This hadn't gone at all as she'd planned. "So this was her plan from the beginning. She's writing a book that will make her father look innocent."

Cull didn't bother to respond to her accusation. "Nikki didn't know Nate was her father until recently," he said, still without looking at her. "I'm sure it's one reason she became interested in the case. But not the only reason."

She stared at him, speechless. How did he know that? *Her grandfather.* He'd talked to her grandfather, which meant he'd been investigating *her.* The irony of it didn't escape her. He'd warned that he would be digging into her life, but she'd thought it was an empty threat.

"Still you have to question her motives," Jim Waters said as he started to sit back down.

"Actually, it's your motives I'm more concerned about, Jim." Travers pushed his wheelchair away from the table. "Why don't we talk about that in my office?"

The attorney had just sat. Now he pushed back up and, looking like a hangdog, followed Travers out of the dining room.

"Why is it that I'm not allowed to mention anything distasteful and he gets to say things like that?" Kitten demanded, getting to her feet and leaving.

"I can't believe you and your father kept this from me," Patricia said to Cull as he tossed down his napkin and turned to Nikki.

"I would imagine you'll have to take that up with my father, Patty. You usually do," he said as he reached for Nikki's hand. "There's something I need to show you in the horse barn."

She stood on rubbery legs. His large hand was warm as it wrapped around hers. She felt that electric thrill at his touch even as she let him lead her out of the dining room. He was angry with her—she could feel it in the no-nonsense way he held her hand all the way to the back door.

"Cull, let me explain," she said as he opened the back door and waited for her to walk through it.

"Not here," was all he said in a low gruff voice.

She swallowed back whatever explanation she'd been about to give and went out the door. She could feel him behind her, hear his boots on the stone path, could almost feel the heat of his anger against her back.

CULL RUED THE day that Patricia had entered their lives for a second time. Their father had remained married to their mother even though she no longer seemed to know him—or her children. Then sixteen years ago, Patty had shown up at the ranch, a baby in her arms and no doubt a sad story to go with it.

Travers McGraw had not just taken her in, he'd divorced his wife and married her. She'd never been a mother to any of them, except Kitten. Admittedly, Cull and his brothers hadn't made it easy for her. He'd resented her intrusion into their lives—and still did.

He reached the barn and turned to find Nikki had followed him as far as the door. She stood silhouetted against it. In the dim light, he couldn't make out her expression, but something about the way she stood made him want to pull her into his arms and hold her.

"I know you're angry," she said quietly.

"Not at you. I knew Patricia had something planned at dinner. All my warnings about not upsetting Dad…" He shook his head.

"How long have you known about my father?" she asked.

"Did you really think I wouldn't check up on you? I made a few calls that first day when I went back into town to get your car."

She took a step toward him. "You talked to my grandfather."

He nodded.

"Why didn't you out me right away?"

Why hadn't he? He'd told his father, who'd taken the news even better than Cull had. "Then she is motivated to solve this even more, isn't she," his father had said. "Don't mention to her that you know. We'll keep it as our little secret for the time being."

"My father asked me not to say anything, but I wouldn't have anyway." He took a step toward her. "If my father had been Nate Corwin, I would try to clear his name, too. It's funny," he said, closing the distance between them. "You seemed…familiar the first time I saw you. There was just something about you. Now I realize what it is. You remind me of your father." He saw that his words pleased her.

"Then you understand why I don't want to believe that your mother and my father…" Her voice broke and she sounded close to tears.

"They were just friends." He brushed a lock of her hair back from her face, his fingertips grazing the soft smooth skin of her cheek. "I'm going to help you find out the truth."

Her eyes widened. "Why?" she asked on a breath.

"Because I liked your father—because I like you." His gaze dropped to her mouth and then his mouth was on hers. He dragged her to him, deepening the kiss as she came willingly into his arms.

Chapter Fifteen

Nikki woke the next morning to a knock on the pool house door. She quickly dressed and went to answer it, hoping it was Cull. She'd had a hard time getting to sleep after The Kiss. Unlike their first kiss, they'd both been into this one. It had sparked a fire to life inside them both. She shuddered to think what they might have done right there in the barn if they hadn't been interrupted.

The memory of that kiss sent a wave of need through her. She'd wanted Cull desperately, but they'd been interrupted by one of the ranch hands who'd apparently needed him more than she did. She hadn't seen him again last night.

Cull had unleashed a desire in her that she hadn't known existed. This morning she had to remind herself that she never mixed business and pleasure. But who was she kidding? She hadn't met anyone who made her interested in dating, let alone losing herself in pleasure.

She opened the door, a smile already on her lips, only to find it wasn't Cull on her doorstep looking worried.

"Ledger?" she said, unable to hide her surprise.

"My father sent me." From his expression, it was clear he wouldn't have been here on his own. "He was surprised you hadn't talked to me yet about the kidnapping."

"I was looking for you yesterday before Cull and I went for a horseback ride."

He nodded as if he'd made himself scarce knowing it was just a matter of time. "Is now a bad time?"

"No." She could see that he wanted to get it over with. "Let's go sit by the pool."

Once they were seated, Nikki put the recorder on the small end table between them. "Let's talk about that night."

"That's just it, I don't remember anything. I was only three."

Nikki nodded, then smiled. "I heard you loved to go outside at night after everyone was asleep." He said nothing. "In fact, when I spoke with Patricia, she told me that you had been outside that night."

His eyes widened in alarm. "Why would she say that? I was in bed asleep."

"I thought you didn't remember?"

"I'm just saying, I must have been in bed asleep." He looked flustered.

"I've already spoken with Cull. He said he awakened that night to find you weren't in your bed. He'd gotten up to go find you when he heard Patricia start screaming." It wasn't exactly what Cull had said, but it was close enough to the truth to hopefully jog Ledger's memory of that night.

He had a faraway, scared look in his eyes. "I told you, I don't remember. But it that's what Cull said…"

"Patricia also told me that when you showed up your bare feet were dirty. She had to wash them before she put you and your brothers into her bed." She let that sink in for a moment. "Does any of this bring back memories?"

He shook his head.

"You'd been outside that night. I think you saw something. Someone. Maybe the kidnapper. Maybe someone carrying away the twins."

He shook his head again and looked away as he shifted in his chair. "I told you—"

"But you saw someone, someone you recognized."

She watched him swallow and look toward

the woods. Her heart began to pound. "Who did you see?"

He started to shake his head. The next words out of his mouth were so soft that she had to lean toward him to hear them. "I saw the bogey-man." He looked up at her, clearly embarrassed. "You see now why I never said anything. I was *three*. Who knows what I saw."

"You saw a man who scared you?"

He nodded. "He came out of the dark pines. He was big and scary."

"Did he see you?"

"No, I hid."

"Where did he go?" she asked, her voice cracking a little.

"Toward the house."

Toward the house. Nikki said nothing for a moment before she asked, "Was he carrying anything when you saw him?"

"No, not that I saw."

"Did you see him again?"

"Not that night," he said, and met her gaze. "I never told. I was too scared. I thought he would come back for me." That long-ago fear made his eyes shine with the terror he'd felt as that three-year-old.

"But you saw him some other time?"

He swallowed and avoided her gaze. "A few days before the kidnapping. He was standing on a street corner in town talking to our cook, Frieda. They seemed to be arguing. He looked up right at me." Ledger shivered. "It was the way he looked at me. But it might not even have been the same man. Another reason I never said anything."

"Did you ever see him again after the kidnapping?"

"No. Only in my nightmares."

"Did you say anything to Frieda?"

He shook his head. "Do you think he was the man who took the twins?"

"I don't know. He didn't have them when you saw him, so probably not," she said, realizing that she wanted to reassure him.

But her heart was pounding. She feared that Ledger's bogeyman had been the kidnapper—before he'd taken the twins.

NIKKI FOUND PATRICIA coming out of the kitchen.

"Whatever it is, I don't have time for it," the woman said in greeting.

As Nikki had come into the house, she'd heard mother and daughter arguing about shopping. Apparently, Patricia was going shopping and wasn't waiting until Kitten got out of school so she could go with her.

"I just need to ask you a few quick questions," she said. "I'm sure your shopping can wait that long."

Patricia gave her a haughty, irritated look, but then glanced toward Travers's office. He was behind his desk and he was watching their discussion. The woman's expression sweetened like saccharine. "I guess I could spare a few minutes."

"Use my office," her husband said and wheeled out from behind his desk. "I'll go see if I can make Kitten feel better."

Patricia let out a low growl as her husband passed, but kept a smile plastered on her face. She sighed as her husband disappeared into the back of the house. "I really don't have time for this."

From what Nikki had seen, all Patricia had was time. She was overdressed for a shopping trip into Whitehorse. Was that really why she was going into town, or was she headed somewhere else? Nikki wondered, catching the sweet scent of the woman's perfume.

"I'll make it quick," Nikki promised as Patty glanced at her watch in clear irritation. She walked behind her husband's desk, but didn't sit.

Nikki took a chair facing her and turned on the recorder and said, "After twenty-five years, maybe there are things you remember that you didn't that night."

"Well, there aren't. We already did this. And I don't want to relive all of it again. I'm sure you also have my testimony that I gave the FBI and sheriff at the time. That should be sufficient. It isn't going to change. Anyway, I don't understand what the point is since we already know what happened that night."

Nikki ignored that. "I can imagine how hard all this has been on you, living under the suspicion and the mystery of what happened to the twins," she said, trying another approach.

"You have no idea what it is has been like for me," Patricia said, her voice breaking. "It isn't just the suspicion. I live in *Marianne's* shadow." She put a world of contempt into that one word as she dropped her voice. "You think it doesn't bother me that Travers goes to see her every day? She's completely loony-bin nuts, doesn't speak, doesn't do anything but rock. Does it make any difference to him? No. He still loves her. He still misses her." She sniffed and looked away toward the window as she folded her arms over her chest. "There are days when I just want to get in my car and drive as far away from here as I can. But where would I go? What would I do? I have Kitten to think about."

Nikki had listened without interrupting, but now she asked, "Why *did* you come back?"

Patricia turned to look at her as if for a few

minutes, she'd forgotten she was there. "I had nowhere to go and Travers had always been kind to me. When I'd left, he told me that I always had a home at Sundown Stallion Station."

"And now you're his wife."

"I didn't come back to marry him, if that's what you're thinking. I was…desperate, if you must know. I'd lost my job and with a baby to support… He was lonely."

"What about Kitten's father?"

"*Travers* is her father."

"Her *biological* father?"

"Of course not," Patricia snapped. "Her biological father was never involved."

Nikki could have argued that point since he was the one who got her pregnant. "You left here soon after the kidnapping."

"It wasn't like I could stay!" Her voice rose to shrill. "Even after Marianne went crazy and Nate Corwin was arrested, everyone still blamed me. I was the *nanny*. How had I let this happen?"

"It must have been hard to come back," Nikki said.

"I guess I thought after almost ten years that things would be different."

"And you had Kitten to think about."

Patricia narrowed her gaze. "You think I came back for Travers's money?"

"You're a lot younger than your husband."

The woman actually smiled. "You and the rest of the county can think whatever you want." She stretched to her full height. "I really don't care. But you'd better not write anything bad about me. If you defame me, I will sue you for everything you have."

"Yes, your husband employs his own lawyer. You must have known Jim Waters when you were the nanny, back when you were nineteen. You also knew Blake Ryan, the ranch manager and close family friend."

Patricia narrowed her eyes. "I don't know what you're getting at," she said, but Nikki was sure she did. "You should be careful making accusations. If I had my way, you wouldn't have gotten near my house, near me or my daughter. I personally am not going to do this anymore, no matter what my husband says." With that, she stalked out. A few moments later, Nikki heard her raising her voice in the kitchen, arguing with her husband and berating Frieda.

But Nikki was going to find out once and for all why Frieda put up with it.

AFTER THE KITCHEN cleared out, with Patricia storming off to town, Kitten taking Travers's car to school and Travers locking himself in his office, Nikki went into the kitchen.

Frieda was hard at work, but she seemed more beaten down than ever this morning.

"I thought Wednesday was your day off?" Nikki asked.

Frieda turned from what she'd been doing. "Patricia had a few things she wanted me to do before I left."

"One of the problems of living under the same roof," Nikki commented. "Well, I really want to go with you to your quilting group. If that's all right." She could see by Frieda's anxious look that it wasn't.

The woman glanced around as if frantically trying to come up with a way out of it. "I wasn't planning to quilt today."

Nikki took a step toward her. "Frieda, I thought it would be nice to get us both out of here. I'd love to see what everyone is working on. We can make it a quick trip."

Frieda looked resigned. "I can finish up here and leave in about thirty minutes then."

"Great, we can take my rental. You can just relax and enjoy the ride."

But even as she said it, Frieda looked anything but relaxed.

She'd just returned to the pool house when there was a knock at her door. She feared it might be Frieda with a better excuse for not going today, but when she opened the door, she found Cull standing there. One look at him and she could tell he was upset.

"You went to the sheriff without mentioning it to me?" he demanded as he pushed his way in, forcing her to step back.

"I'm worried about your father. I would think you would be, too. I didn't want to say anything to anyone else since it was just a suspicion and I knew you'd get upset."

He pulled off his Stetson to rake a hand through his thick hair. All the fight seemed to go out of him. "My father just told me about the sheriff coming by the hospital before he was released to take a hair sample. You can't think that she's poisoning him."

Of course that was exactly what she thought. "It can't be much of a reach for you since you didn't even ask who I suspected—and neither did the sheriff."

"If true, Patty can't possibly think she can get away with it," he said.

"Why not, if she got away with it before?" Nikki said as she walked into the small pool house kitchen. "Coffee? I made a pot this morning."

He nodded and joined her in the small space. "What are you talking about—she did it before?"

"I don't just suspect she is poisoning your father. I think she did the same thing to your mother in the weeks leading up to the kidnapping."

He stared at her as she poured him a cup.

"Think about it. Your mother was acting… strangely. What if it wasn't postpartum depression at all? What if she was acting the way she was because she was being poisoned? I know it seems like a stretch but when I saw your father and how he looked…" She handed him his cup of coffee and poured one for herself.

"If what you're saying is true…"

"It's just a suspicion at this point. That's why I went to the sheriff. Hopefully when the lab test comes back, it will prove that I'm wrong."

"Or right."

Motioning to a chair, she sat down and Cull did the same.

He seemed lost in thought. "You do realize that if you're right, I'm going to kill her."

"No, you're not. You're not a killer."

He met her gaze. "You sure about that?"

"Yes." Was she basing that on the kiss? Or something more?

Cull swore under his breath. "You're right, but I'm going to want to."

"Did the sheriff say when they'd have lab results?"

"She said she'd marked them a priority and would get back to us."

"What did your father say?" Nikki had to ask.

"He was upset, of course. He defended her, but not very strongly. It made me wonder if he suspected something. What man wants to admit, though, that his spouse is poisoning him?"

"We don't know that's the case."

"Yet," Cull said. "McCall told me the symptoms of long-term arsenic poisoning. I can understand why you thought of it. I'm sorry I didn't."

"I have a suspicious mind, and murder is kind of my business."

He met her gaze. "I've noticed that. What now?"

"I continue gathering information. I still have to talk to Tilly and Frieda. They both were live-in staff at the time of the kidnapping." She didn't tell him that she especially wanted to talk to Frieda after what Ledger had told her about his "bogeyman."

THE SHERIFF HAD asked the lab to put a rush on the hair samples. She'd never been good at waiting. She especially wasn't now.

Her husband had called from Winchester Ranch to tell her that her grandmother and mother weren't at each other's throats and that their daughter was enjoying being around the grandmas.

"How are *you* doing?" she asked him.

"I forget how pretty it is out here. And lunch was good."

Luke always tried to see the good in everything. It was incredibly annoying. But she smiled in spite of herself.

"I'm waiting for the lab to bring me results. A case of a husband possibly being poisoned by his wife."

"Yikes. I'd better check your mother. I wouldn't put it past your grandmother to put something in her food."

She knew he was kidding, but still it worried her. Her grandmother wasn't the most patient person and the bad blood between her and McCall's mother, Ruby, ran blood-spilling deep.

"I'm kidding," her husband said. "You sound too serious on your end of the phone."

"You can hear that?"

"Because I know you so well," he said. "I love you."

"I love you."

"Hope you get the lab tests soon. What will you do if they come back positive for poison?" he asked. "Do you have enough for an arrest?"

"Not yet. The next step will be to get a warrant to search the house."

"Sounds like that's what you're expecting."

McCall realized it was. "If true, it gets complicated. This might not be the first time this woman has systematically poisoned someone to get rid of them."

Chapter Sixteen

Unable to sit still after Cull left, Nikki found Tilly running the vacuum in the off-limits wing. She called her name, but the older woman didn't hear her. Matilda "Tilly" Marks had been twenty-five, married and in debt the year the twins were kidnapped.

Now at fifty, she was divorced and still in debt. Nikki knew that the sheriff and FBI had done a thorough investigation of everyone in the house that night—including Tilly and her husband. They'd found nothing.

"Tilly?" Nikki raised her voice over the whine of the vacuum as she approached the woman. *"Tilly!"*

The sunlight coming in the window seemed to turn the woman's bleached blond hair white. With a start, she realized that it was this white-haired woman she'd seen at this window.

"Tilly?" When she still didn't hear her, she touched the housekeeper's arm.

The poor woman jumped a foot, making Nikki feel terrible.

"I'm sorry," she mouthed as Tilly fumbled to turn off the vacuum. In the silence that fell, she repeated, "I'm sorry. I didn't mean to scare you."

Tilly held her hand over her heart as if to still it. She was a short thin nondescript woman with bottle blond hair and manicured nails. She moved through the house like a ghost, paying little attention to anyone and vice versa, from what Nikki had seen.

"I need to ask you about the night of the kidnapping. Could you take a break for a few minutes?"

Tilly nodded. "I could use a cigarette. Can we step outside?"

Nikki followed the woman to the end of the hall and down the stairs. If the kidnapper wasn't already in the house that night, he could have come in through this entrance. The stairs led down to a small patio next to the woods. Anyone coming in this way wouldn't have been seen.

But in order to get in, someone would have had to leave the door unlocked.

Nikki let the woman light her cigarette and

take a drag before she asked, "What can you tell me about that night?"

"Not much. I had a cold and had taken some medicine so I could sleep. Plus I wear earplugs. I didn't hear a thing until I was awakened by someone pounding on my door. It was a sheriff's deputy. That's when I found out what had happened."

"Where was your room?"

"At the other end of the wing from where the twins were taken," she said, and tilted her head back as she blew out smoke.

"So you were in the room next to Frieda's."

Something in the way Tilly nodded caught her attention. "You would have been able to hear her leave her room."

"Under normal circumstances, but like I said, I took cold medicine that night."

"But you'd heard her come and go other nights," Nikki said, fishing for whatever it was Tilly wasn't saying.

"Sure. I heard her and whoever else come and go."

She took a not-so-wild guess. "A man?"

Tilly shrugged.

"Who was he?"

"A no 'count. I tried to warn her, but she didn't listen. I knew him. I told her he was going to break her heart."

Nikki was still reeling from the fact that Tilly was telling her that Frieda had a man visitor in her room. "Was it all right for her to have a man in her room?"

"Not hardly. Mrs. McGraw, the first Mrs., was very strict about that. Frieda could have been fired, but I wasn't about to tell on her. I got the impression that it was the first man she'd ever...dated, if you know what I mean. She was thirty-nine and never been kissed until him. So, of course, she fell hard."

"Was he a big man? Kind of scary looking?"

Tilly laughed. "Not exactly handsome or bright either."

"So Frieda snuck him in? Did you tell the sheriff and FBI about this?"

The housekeeper put out her cigarette in the dirt, pocketed the stub and lit another with trembling fingers. "He wasn't in her room that night, so why mention it?"

Nikki stared at her. "How do you know that if you were knocked out with cold medicine?"

Tilly sighed. "Because I had a talk with him. Like I said, I knew him. I knew he was using her. I didn't like him in the house at night. He was a bum. I thought he might steal something."

"Like the McGraws twins?"

"No, he wasn't that ambitious or that smart to pull something like that off. I was trying to protect Frieda. So I told him I was going to tell Mr. McGraw and the next time he snuck into the house, he'd be facing a shotgun. That did the trick. Never saw him again."

"Still you had taken the cold medicine—"

"Before I went to bed, before I took the medicine, I heard Frieda in her room pacing. It was late. He hadn't shown up. I knew she'd be disappointed, but it was for the best."

"He could have entered the house after you went to bed."

She shook her head as she took a drag on her cigarette and blew out smoke. "I made sure the door was locked. As I came back up, I saw that her light was out. I could hear her crying. She knew he wasn't going to come by."

Nikki took in this information. "What is this man's name?"

"Harold Cline, but like I said, I never saw him again and neither did Frieda. He left town."

"You don't think it's strange that he disappeared about the same time as the kidnapping?"

"He probably thought he'd be blamed for it once Frieda told the sheriff that she'd been letting him in at night."

"But Frieda must not have told, otherwise wouldn't she have been let go?"

Tilly seemed to consider that. "I suppose you're right."

"And that's the same reason *you* never told."

The housekeeper suddenly looked worried. "You aren't going to tell Mr. McGraw. At my age it's impossible to find another job." Was that what Frieda thought, as well?

"No." If there was something to this lead, then it could come out when the book did. In the meantime…

Tilly seemed to relax. "Like I said, Harold wasn't smart enough to pull off the kidnapping and if he had, he would have spent the money. The ransom money never turned up, right?"

"Right." Still, Nikki wanted to know more about Harold Cline.

CULL FOUND HIS father in his office. "I hope you aren't working."

Travers smiled up at him. "I'm not. I've always liked this room. I feel comfortable in here." The phone rang. He motioned to Cull to give him a minute and answered.

"No, Patricia, I can't tell Frieda that. It's her day off. She told me that she and Nikki are going to visit her quilting group. You have to stop making her work on her day off. Fine. Whatever." He hung up and sighed.

Cull saw that his father was upset. He wanted to wring Patricia's neck.

"I'm going to see Mother. I thought you might like to go with me."

"I can't. Jim Waters will be stopping by. I need to talk to him."

Cull studied his father. "Tell me you're going to fire him."

His father chuckled. "He's been with me a long time."

Travers believed in rewarding loyalty. "Maybe too long." He turned toward the door. "I'll tell Mother hello for you."

"Thank you. Tell her...tell her I still love her."

Cull nodded and left, his thoughts veering from one to the next and always coming back to Nikki. He'd fought his attraction to her, but it was so much more than that. The woman fascinated him. He'd never met anyone like her. If only they had met under other circumstances.

AT THE HOSPITAL, he let a nurse lead him down to his mother's room. Marianne McGraw was right where he expected her to be—in her rocking chair holding the two worn dolls. She didn't react when he pulled up a chair and sat down in front of her. The blank eyes stared straight ahead, unseeing.

"Hello, Mother," he said. "It's Cull. Dad wanted me to tell you that he still loves you. Also I thought you'd want to know that he had a heart attack." Did her rocking change? "He's okay though. Weak, but recovering."

He listened to the steady creak of the rocker for a few moments. "I met someone." He let out a chuckle. "After all this time I meet someone who interests me and she ends up being a true crime writer doing a book on the kidnapping. But I guess we can't help the people we fall for, huh."

The admission surprised him, but had no effect on his mother.

He talked for another ten minutes, telling her about the ranch, the new stallion, her other children.

"Ledger is still in love with Abby," he said with a sigh. "I can't see any way that can have a happy ending." Just like his own situation, he thought. "Boone, well, he's ornery enough that it will take a special woman to turn his head."

He watched his mother's blank expression as she rocked back and forth, the rocker creaking with her movement. "This woman who's staying at the ranch, the true crime writer, she thinks she can find out what really happened that night. A part of me hopes it's true. But another part of me…" He swallowed, surprised at the fear that filled him. "What if she finds out that it was you? You and Nate? I don't believe it. But if it turns out I'm wrong… I can't let that happen, Mother. But I'm not sure I can stop her. I don't think anyone can."

THE SHERIFF HAD just gotten back from a meeting when she saw that she had a message from the lab. She quickly dialed the number and was handed off to the lab tech who'd taken the test.

"You have the results?" she said in the phone. McCall wasn't sure what she expected to hear. That Nikki St. James was wrong. Or that it was true and there was someone in that house systematically poisoning Travers McGraw. She'd been in law enforcement long enough that nothing should surprise her.

"We found arsenic in the hair follicles," the lab tech said.

McCall let out the breath she'd been holding. So it was true. "Thank you. Please have those results sent to my office." She started to hang up, but instead disconnected and dialed a judge she had a good working relationship with.

"I'm going to need a warrant," she told him and quickly informed him of the lab test. Poison had always been a woman's weapon throughout history.

"I'll have your warrant within the hour," the judge promised. "I'm assuming you have a suspect?"

Everyone in the county knew Patricia Owens

McGraw. She could count the number of people who she'd befriended on one hand. "Let's just hope she doesn't know we're on to her. I'd like to wrap this one up quickly. The media is going to have a field day."

"Yes," the judge agreed. "Especially with the anniversary of the kidnapping only days away."

She hung up, thinking about Nikki St. James. The woman was sharp. She just might have saved Travers McGraw's life. But the irony didn't escape McCall. If Nikki discovered through her investigation for her book that the twins were dead, it might kill him given his condition.

NIKKI HAD FOUND out what she could about Harold Cline before she returned to the kitchen to find Frieda finishing her chores.

Just as Tilly had told her, Harold had been a ne'er-do-well with a sketchy background. He'd done poorly in school, had trouble holding jobs, had been married and divorced, but had never had a run-in with the law.

She had to agree with Tilly that he didn't look like someone who could engineer one of the most famous kidnappings in Montana history and get away with it. But whoever had taken the twins had help, and that person could have been the mastermind behind the kidnapping. Harold Cline could have just been the muscle.

The fact that Harold Cline seemed to have dropped off the face of the earth right after the kidnapping also made Nikki suspicious. She couldn't find anywhere in the information she'd gotten on the case that the sheriff or FBI had talked to Harold. Either they hadn't known about him or didn't consider him a suspect. She was betting it was the former.

Which was why she was anxious to talk to Frieda away from Patricia's prying eyes and ears.

The cook took off her apron and still seemed to hesitate. "I'm not staying at the Whitehorse Sewing Circle today. I'm just dropping off some fabric for future quilts. We make quilts for new babies in the area." She stopped short as if she hadn't meant to say that much.

"Great, I'll get my car. You can tell me where to go."

Frieda looked resigned as she climbed into the passenger side of the rental car a few minutes later, hugging the bag of fabric.

"I thought this would give us a chance to talk without any interruptions," Nikki said once they were on the road.

The cook said nothing as she looked out the side window.

She drove south, away from Whitehorse, deeper into the Missouri Breaks, following Frieda's directions. "I'm surprised they meet this far from Whitehorse."

"The first settlement of Whitehorse was actually nearer the Missouri River," Frieda said. "But when the railroad came through, the town migrated five miles to the north, taking the name with it. So now, it's called Old Town. It's little more than a ghost town, though some families have remained." Again she stopped abruptly.

Nikki drove through rolling prairie, the purple outline of the Little Rockies off to their right, before she dropped over a hill and slowed at a rusted sign warning there were children at play. A tumbleweed cartwheeled across the road in front of the rental. Frieda was right about Old Town being a ghost town. There were a few buildings still standing, including what appeared to have once been a country schoolhouse.

"It's that large building on the right," Frieda said as they passed the old school yard and she saw a weathered sign on the next building that read Old Town Whitehorse Community Center.

There were three pickups parked out front. Nikki pulled in next to the one on the end and shut off the engine.

"Looks like the whole group is here," Frieda said. She suddenly seemed even more nervous.

"If you prefer I not come in…" Nikki said.

"I just need to drop this fabric off." The cook looked conflicted. "You might as well come in and see what they're working on today."

As they stepped inside, Nikki was hit with a scent that reminded her of the old trunk in her mother's attic where she'd found the newspaper clippings about Nate Corwin.

It took a moment for her eyes to adjust to the cool dimness inside. Three older women sat around a quilting hoop. They all turned, their hands holding the needles and thread hovering above the fabric.

"I brought a guest," Frieda announced into the deathly silence.

The women quickly welcomed Nikki, though they seemed to watch her with interest.

"This is Nikki St. James. She's a true crime writer. She's doing a story on the McGraw kidnapping," Frieda blurted and took a breath.

"So we heard," said a small gray-haired woman with bright blue eyes. "It's a small town. Do you quilt?"

"No," Nikki said as she watched the woman make tiny perfect stitches in what appeared to be a baby quilt. "My neighbor does. I have one of her quilts. I love it."

"Did Frieda tell you that we have been quilting here for years? Used to make a quilt for every newborn in the area. Now not so much," the woman said almost wistfully. "Our numbers have dropped considerably."

Nikki had done her homework and found out that along with quilting the women of the Whitehorse Sewing Circle had also placed babies out for adoption illegally since the 1930s. No one had seen any jail time since most of the "leaders" behind the illegal adoptions were dead now.

"So tell us about your book," a large white-haired woman inquired.

"Not much to tell," Nikki admitted. "I've just begun my interviews."

Frieda hugged the bag of fabric she'd brought. "Has she interviewed you?" a sour-face dyed redhead asked Frieda.

"Why would she? I have nothing to add," Frieda said without looking at Nikki.

"I'm sure Frieda will help if she can. We all want to know what happened to the twins," Nikki said, hoping it was true.

"Well, most of us already know," the sour-faced one said. "One look at Marianne McGraw tells the whole story."

The three women who'd been at the table when Nikki had entered all shook their heads as if in condolence to poor Marianne. "Imagine the nightmares that woman has," the sweet little gray-haired woman said in sympathy.

"Of course there's a chance she wasn't involved," Nikki said.

Sour-face scoffed.

"There is always a chance that new information will surface," Nikki said and all the women gave her a look of pity.

"That good-looking horse trainer turned Marianne McGraw's head. It happens all the time and look how it ended," said the bottle redhead. "They both got what they had coming."

"But what about those sweet babies?" the little gray-haired woman said.

"They're long dead," sour-face snapped. "Someone will stumble onto their graves one of these days, you'll see. Lucky the kidnappers are dead or locked up. Otherwise, it would be dangerous digging around in the past for your book."

Next to Nikki, Frieda dropped the bag of fabric she'd been holding. "I'm so clumsy," she said, sounding close to tears.

They all turned to look at her as she quickly retrieved it from the floor and put it on a nearby table. All the color had washed from her face. For a moment Nikki was afraid the cook might faint. What had the women said that had upset her?

"We should go and let you ladies get back to work," Frieda said. She had regained some composure, but clearly didn't look well as they said their goodbyes and left.

Nikki thought about what Patricia had said to Frieda about the quilt group, how the cook had gotten upset that day, as well. But what was it about this group of older women quilting?

"Are you all right?" Nikki had asked as she started the car.

"I just remembered something I promised Mrs. McGraw I would do today."

"I thought it was your day off," Nikki reminded her.

"Since I started living on the ranch, Mrs. McGraw gets confused about what days I'm actually off," Frieda said, turning away to look out the side window.

Nikki backed out onto the dirt road. "Whose idea was it for you to move in?"

"The first Mrs. McGraw thought it would save me time driving back and forth from Whitehorse and save me money on a rental when I spent most of my time at the ranch anyway. It was a kind gesture on her part since my husband, George, is a truck driver who spends a lot of time on the road."

Unlike Patricia, who treated her like her private servant, Nikki thought. "I'm surprised you've stayed with the McGraws all these years," she said carefully as she drove away from Old Town.

She couldn't shake the feeling that Patricia was holding something over Frieda. Why else would the cook put up with the way the woman treated her?

Frieda remained quiet.

"Patricia must be a hard woman to work for." Still nothing. Nikki looked over at her. "Frieda, either you are working on sainthood or Patty is holding something over you. Which is it?"

All the color drained from Frieda's face again. "I don't know what…you're talking about," she stammered.

"Given the way she treats you and how wonderfully you cook, why haven't you quit? I know there are other ranches that would snatch you up in a heartbeat." Nikki looked over at the woman in her passenger seat.

"I can't leave Mr. McGraw. Or the boys," she mumbled, and looked embarrassed.

Nikki thought that might have something to do with it, but not everything. "You know what I think? I think the woman is holding something over your head. I think it might have something to do with a man. Wouldn't you feel better to get it off your chest? To get her off your back?"

She let out a bitter chuckle. "You have no idea."

"Let me help you," Nikki said.

Frieda merely stared out the side window.

Nikki's attention was drawn away from the woman as she caught movement in the rearview mirror. She'd been driving down the dirt road through the wild country and hadn't seen another car the whole way.

Now, though, an old rusty truck had come roaring up behind her. Nikki looked for a place to pull off, but there was nothing but a ditch on both sides of the road. She sped up a little since she had been going slow.

The truck stayed right with her, riding her bumper. She couldn't see the driver because of the glare off the cracked windshield of the truck.

Frieda had noticed something was wrong. She sat up and was watching in her side mirror. "I was afraid this would happen," she said, her voice breaking with fear. "He's going to kill us."

Nikki shot her a surprised look. What was she talking about? "No one's going to kill us."

"You have no idea what you've done by coming here, asking all these questions, digging up the past," Frieda said, sounding close to tears.

"What have I done?" she asked, speeding up as she looked ahead for a place to pull over so the truck could pass.

The woman shook her head. She looked like a woman of seventy, her blonde hair appearing gray, worry making her face look haggard.

"Frieda, I've known something was wrong since I got here. You can tell me."

The woman turned to look at her, eyes shimmering with tears. "I knew it would come out one day. It isn't like I ever thought…" Her voice broke.

Nikki couldn't see a place to pull over and the truck driver seemed determined to get past even though there was only the one lane and no shoulder to pull off on.

"This has something to do with Harold Cline, doesn't it? The reason you let Patricia treat you so badly."

Frieda let out a cry and covered her face with both hands as the pickup slammed into the back of the rental car. "I told you he was going to kill us."

Fighting to keep the rental car on the narrow road, Nikki demanded, "Who is that driving the truck?"

Frieda said nothing and hunkered on her side of the car as the truck came up fast and crashed into them again.

The back of the rental fishtailed and for a moment Nikki feared she would lose control. "Get your cell phone out. Call the sheriff!" Frieda didn't move. "Frieda!"

They were coming to one of the rolling hills and a curve. Nikki hated to go any faster but she had no choice. She pushed down on the accelerator, hoping to outrun the truck. But the driver must have anticipated her plan.

The truck came up with so much speed that when it hit the back of the rental there was no controlling it any longer. The car tires caught a rut and the next thing Nikki knew they were sideways in the road. But not for long.

The tires caught another rut and she felt the car tilt.

"Hang on!" she cried as the rental car went off the road and over the edge of the hillside. It rolled once, then again and again until it came to rest at the bottom of the hill in a gully.

Chapter Seventeen

"Is there a problem?" Cull asked as he glanced to where Patricia was slamming pots and pans around in the kitchen, before he took a stool at the breakfast bar. Kitten had her head in the refrigerator.

"Frieda isn't back to make dinner. I'm going to fire her. I've put up with that woman long enough."

"It's her day off," Cull said, but Patricia didn't seem to hear. She appeared nervous and overly upset over something that happened once a week. Usually, though, Frieda gave in and cooked.

"Do we have any celery?" Kitten was asking. "You think it's true that it takes more calories to eat celery than it has in it?"

Cull didn't bother to respond. "Have you seen Nikki?" he asked even though he knew that would be a sore subject and the woman was already in a foul mood.

"She took off with Frieda," Kitten said, coming out from behind the refrigerator door with a stalk of celery in her hand.

Patricia slammed down a pot. "Who knows what that fool woman might tell her about all of us."

"I hope you aren't planning to cook or we are all going to starve," Cull said. "Or wish we did," he added under his breath. "So where did Nikki go with Frieda?"

"To that old lady quilt group," Kitten said between bites of celery.

Patricia cussed under her breath and looked at her watch. "Shouldn't they be back by now?"

Having enough of this, Cull headed toward the living room. Looking up, he saw the sheriff and two deputies coming down the stairs. They headed toward his father's office. Travers McGraw was behind his desk. He looked as if he'd aged in the last few minutes.

"What's happened?" Cull demanded, his heart in his throat. Had there been an accident? Was it one of his brothers? Was it their mother? Was it… His pulse began to pound. Nikki? With a start he saw that one of the deputies was carrying what appeared to be an evidence bag.

Cull realized that the lab tests must have come back—and that Nikki had been right.

"Where is your stepmother?" Travers asked as he came out of his office. McCall gave him a nod, and Cull saw the pain in his father's expression before he answered.

"She's in the kitchen with Kitten. I don't believe she heard you arrive." The sheriff and deputies started in that direction. "Please don't handcuff her. Not in front of her daughter," Travers said.

Cull turned to his father. "It's *true*? She's been poisoning you?"

He nodded. "Just as we suspect she did your mother twenty-five years ago."

"Patricia McGraw?" he heard the sheriff ask.

From his vantage point, Cull watched as Patty turned. Her eyes widened as she looked from the sheriff to the deputies and past them to her husband.

"If you could step out into the living room," the sheriff said to her.

Patty looked as if she wanted to make a run for it. "What is this about?"

"If you could please ask your daughter to stay in here," the sheriff said as she took Patty's arm and led her out of the kitchen.

Kitten started to follow, but Travers wheeled

past the deputy to keep her in the kitchen. "What is going on with Mother?" the teen demanded.

The sheriff was saying, "Patricia Owens McGraw, you're under arrest for attempted murder. You have the right to remain silent..." McCall continued reading the Miranda rights as Patty argued that she didn't know what the sheriff was talking about.

One of the deputies showed her something they'd found upstairs. Arsenic? Cull hoped they put her *under* the jail. If all of Nikki's suspicions were true... He fisted his hands at his side.

"Call my lawyer!" she barked at Cull as she was handcuffed, a lawman holding each of her elbows as they steered her toward the front door. "Call Jim. It's all a mistake. That poison was planted in my room."

"No one said we found it in your room," the sheriff said.

"It's all lies! I'm being framed! It's that writer. She did this!" Patricia looked over her shoulder at Cull. "Why would I poison your father? I love him."

"Where are they taking my mother?" Kitten cried as she tried to get past her stepfather's wheelchair. A moment later, the front door closed, car engines revved and Travers rolled out of the kitchen with a crying Kitten.

Ledger and Boone both came in then, both

looking worried. No doubt they'd seen the sheriff's patrol cars out front and Patricia being led away.

"I'll explain everything," Travers said as he asked them all to sit down. Cull listened as his father explained that lab tests had been taken of his hair. Patricia had been poisoning him for some time, which no doubt was why he'd been so sick.

"Not just sick. She almost killed you!" Boone cried. "How did you figure it out?"

"Nikki St. James suspected it and went to the sheriff," their father said.

Cull glanced at his watch, worry burrowing in his belly. "Kitten said that Nikki and Frieda had gone out to Old Town." His father nodded. "Shouldn't they have been back by now? I'm going to drive down there. Let me know if you hear from Nikki," he said and he was out the door and driving toward Old Town Whitehorse.

NIKKI CAME TO SLOWLY, as if she'd either been stunned or knocked unconscious. For a moment, she didn't know where she was or what had happened. It came back to her in a rush. To her surprise, the car had landed right side up in a gully.

She looked over at Frieda, who thankfully appeared to be shaken but not injured. "Are you all right?"

The woman nodded. "You're bleeding."

Nikki touched her temple, her fingers coming away wet with blood. "I'm all right," she said, more to assure herself than Frieda as she dug out her cell phone. She prayed there would be enough coverage out here to get the sheriff. She looked back up the hillside they had rolled down, half expecting to see the pickup truck idling there.

The road above them appeared to be empty.

Nikki was glad to see she had a few bars on her phone and quickly tapped in 9-1-1. When the dispatcher answered, she told her what had happened. "I'm not sure exactly where we are."

"Near Alkali Creek," Frieda said.

She gave this information to the dispatcher. "No, I don't think we need an ambulance. But please hurry." She disconnected and tried to open her door. It was jammed. She thought she smelled gas. "Can you get your door open?"

Frieda didn't seem to hear her. She'd begun to cry.

Nikki reached across her to open the passenger-side door. "We need to get out of the car, Frieda."

As if in a fugue state, the cook climbed out, staggering against the hillside before sitting down hard. Nikki climbed out the passenger side and reached for Frieda's hand.

"We need to get away from the car. Gas is leaking out. I don't think it is going to blow, but it could catch fire. Do you hear me?" She stared at the woman, worried that maybe she was injured more than she'd first thought.

When she looked up at Nikki, there were tears in her eyes. "I told you he would kill us."

She took Frieda's hand and pulled her up, leading her away from the car to an outcropping of rock before letting her sit down again.

"He'll come back," Frieda said. "He can't let us live. He thinks we know too much."

"Who?"

The cook shook her head. She could see that the woman was terrified. Nikki had been so focused on making sure Frieda was all right and getting them away from the car that she hadn't let the full weight of what had happened register.

"Frieda, if you know who that was who ran us off the road, you need to tell me. Does this have something to do with the kidnapping? Frieda, talk to me. I can help you. Whatever is going on, you can't keep it to yourself anymore. This is serious."

"It's all my fault," the cook said and began to sob.

Nikki was trying to imagine Frieda being part of the kidnapping. The woman *had* been living in the house at the time of the kidnapping and could have drugged the babies and then handed them out the window to her boyfriend, Harold Cline. But that would mean that Frieda had been the mastermind behind the plot. That seemed doubtful.

"Frieda, please tell me. Whatever it is—"

"I was thirty-nine. *Thirty-nine!* Old enough to know better."

Nikki guessed at once that she was talking about Harold Cline. She felt her skin prickle. She tried to keep her voice calm, consoling. "You fell in love?"

She seemed surprised that Nikki had guessed. "He was funny, made me laugh, and he really seemed to like me."

Nikki feared what was coming. "You thought you'd found the man for you," she said instead of asking what the man had conned her into doing.

"I would have done anything for him."

And did, Nikki feared. She wanted to ask but waited as patiently as she could for the rest of the story to come out. She could still smell gas leaking from the car nearby and wondered if they should move farther away, but didn't want to interrupt Frieda now that she had her talking.

"I would sneak him into the house at night," Frieda said between tearful jags. "He'd come to my room and…" She looked away. "He wasn't the only one sneaking in at night."

Nikki thought of her father.

"Patty had her own boyfriend."

She felt another wave of relief wash over her as she thought about the argument she'd witnessed the first night. "Jim Waters? Or Blake Ryan."

"Blake."

"Is it still going on?" she had to ask.

The older woman merely gave her a look.

"So you left the door open on the night of the kidnapping," Nikki guessed, still not sure yet where this was going.

Frieda began to cry again. "He didn't show up. I was so stupid. I really thought he was the one."

"Did you see him again after that night?" Nikki asked.

The woman only cried harder.

She took a breath, warning herself to tread softly. "Patty found out you'd been letting him in." It wasn't a question. It had to be what Patricia was now holding over the cook's head. Unless it had something to do with the kidnapping. "Did she tell the sheriff and FBI about your boyfriend?"

Another look that said she hadn't.

Nikki's heart began to pound. "I don't understand why Patty didn't tell the sheriff and FBI. Unless she was already using it against you." She glanced over at Frieda and saw that was exactly what Patty had been doing.

Patty had known the man was sneaking in and was using it against Frieda even twenty-five years ago. But if the sheriff and FBI found out that Patty had known all this before the kidnapping, then she would be under even more suspicion than she had been at the time, so she'd kept her mouth shut and used it to keep Frieda under her thumb.

"She said she was protecting me and that I owed her," Frieda said between sobs.

Nikki had thought she couldn't dislike Patricia more, but she'd been wrong. How could Patricia keep something like that quiet all these years? Even now, it would be Frieda's word against the new Mrs. McGraw's.

"Was this man ever questioned by the authorities?" Nikki had to ask even though she knew the answer already, if indeed Frieda's lover had been Harold Cline, as Tilly had told her.

Frieda shook her head as she wiped at her tears. "I don't care what the sheriff does to me. I deserve it, but do you have to put it in your book?"

"I won't put in anything until I have the whole story."

That seemed to relieve Frieda. "I never told. Marianne was already locked up and so was the horse trainer. I figured they had the kidnappers and that it wasn't my...lover."

"I'm going to need to know the name of the man, Frieda."

She hesitated but only a moment. "Harold Cline."

Her mind was racing as she tried to understand what it was Frieda was telling her—and wasn't telling her. "You'd want to know why he hadn't shown that night. Maybe he'd seen the horse trainer stealing the babies," Nikki said. "You would have gone to see him."

Frieda looked away again.

Nikki felt her heart sink. Tilly was wrong about one thing. Harold Cline had kidnapped the twins and Frieda knew it. Knew it because she'd seen him with the babies?

She was frantically trying to put the pieces together. Frieda had said it was all her fault. "Was there any reason to fear for the twins' safety in that house twenty-five years ago?"

"You don't know what the first Mrs. McGraw was like then. She was confused all the time. Often she couldn't remember the names of her children. I overheard her say that she didn't want the twins, wanted nothing to do with them and wished they would disappear."

A piece of the puzzle dropped into place. "You shared this information with your boyfriend."

Frieda let out a sob. "I had no idea he would kidnap the twins."

There it was. Harold Cline had taken the twins. "That's why you feel so guilty." But when she saw Frieda's expression, she knew that telling him about Marianne's state of mind wasn't the only reason Frieda felt guilty. Her heart dropped.

"Your boyfriend must have thought he was saving them," Nikki said, hoping to keep the cook talking. "That they would get better homes." But why not take the kidnapping ransom money and let the twins be found alive and well? Why make them disappear?

She thought about the broken rung on the ladder and the concern that the kidnapper had fallen, injuring one or both of the babies.

What other reason would the kidnapper have for not returning the babies?

"He did plan to find them good homes, right?"

Frieda's eyes filled with tears again.

She heard the sound of a vehicle. Shouldn't the sheriff be here by now? What if Frieda was right and the man who'd tried to run them off the road had come back?

She looked around for a place they might hide and saw nothing but short scrub pine and sage-brush.

"Maybe I should call the sheriff again," she said to Frieda, but the woman didn't seem to hear her. Nikki realized that the key pieces of the puzzle were still missing.

"Where is Harold Cline now?" she asked as she started to dig her cell phone out of her pocket. Frieda had said that "he" would kill them. "Is Harold Cline the man who ran us off the road?"

"No," Frieda said her voice cold and hard. "He's dead. I killed him."

CULL TOOK A shortcut to Old Town and arrived at the Whitehorse Community Center as several older women were coming out.

He looked around for Nikki's rental car, but didn't see it. "Was Frieda here?" he asked a small gray-haired woman.

"Earlier, she and the writer. They left a long time ago, though."

He thanked her and headed down the main road thinking he must have missed them by taking the shortcut. Patricia's arrest had thrown him. He was still trying to process the fact that she'd been systematically poisoning his father—

and might have done the same thing twenty-five years ago to his mother.

A feeling of doom had come over him when he'd realized that Frieda and Nikki should have been back to the ranch a good hour ago.

Maybe it was seeing his mother this morning, but he kept thinking that Nikki was right. If Patty had been poisoning his mother twenty-five years ago, it would explain her behavior more than postpartum depression. It could also explain her breakdown and how quickly she'd gone downhill. Losing the twins must have been the last straw.

But if it was true, would the sheriff be able to prove that Marianne was a victim of Patty's, and so was her husband? He wished he could get his hands around Patty's throat. He would choke the truth out of her.

The arrest had happened so quickly that he hadn't had time to think—let alone react. Now he was furious. Patty could have killed his father. Travers had taken it better than Cull would have. What wife poisoned her husband?

His cell phone rang. He answered, surprised he could get service this far out. "Hello?"

"A call just came in over the scanner," his brother Ledger told him. "A car was run off the road near Alkali Creek. Isn't that on the way to Old Town?"

"Who put in the call to the sheriff?" Cull asked and held his breath.

"Nikki St. James. She said she and Frieda weren't hurt. Deputies are on the way. They got held up because of Patricia's arrest. Where are you?"

"On my way to Alkali Creek," he said, and disconnected.

Cull hadn't gone far when he saw the tracks. He slowed. There was broken glass from a headlight at the edge of the road. Ahead he saw more tracks and in the distance, a dark green pickup parked off the road.

He had his window down as he drove toward the tracks. He hadn't gone far when he heard the gunshot.

NIKKI WAS STUNNED by Frieda's confession. So stunned that it took a moment to realize what was happening. There was a sound like something hard hitting stone. At the same time, Frieda flinched and let out a soft cry.

When she looked over at the woman sitting with her back against a large rock, Nikki saw that Frieda was holding a hand over her stomach. It took her a wild moment to realize that blood was oozing out from between her fingers.

The second rifle shot pinged off the rock above Nikki's head. She scrambled up, grabbed hold of Frieda and dragged her around the rock outcropping. Again she heard the sound of a vehicle engine.

She fumbled out her cell phone and quickly punched in 9-1-1 again, telling the dispatcher what had happened.

"An ambulance is on the way," she told Frieda as she disconnected.

The woman was still breathing, but her breaths were shallow and she was clearly in a lot of pain. Nikki had stanched the bleeding as much as she could with her jacket.

Her mind was racing.

"I can't die yet. I can't die with this on my conscience."

"You're not going to die."

A crooked smile curled her lips. "When I heard that someone had taken the twins, I knew."

"Frieda, you shouldn't try to talk."

The woman didn't seem to hear her. "I prayed it wasn't him. But when I couldn't reach him… There was an old cabin in the Little Rockies that Harold used during hunting season. I knew the ransom had been paid, but the babies still hadn't been returned." She grimaced in pain, her voice choked with tears as she said, "He was digging a hole to bury them when I found him."

Nikki felt her heart drop like a stone. She couldn't breathe, couldn't speak.

"He said it was my fault. I'm the one who said the twins weren't safe and he was just doing what I wanted him to do. The babies were in a burlap bag on the ground next to the hole he'd been digging. I begged him to take them back."

Hope soared at her words. "Take them back? They were still alive?"

Still Frieda didn't seem to hear her. She was lost in the past, lost in telling a secret hard kept all these years. "He said, 'Have you lost your mind? The place is crawling with cops. And what would I say? Yes, I took the little snots, but I've decided to return them because Frieda has changed her mind? You're in this as deep as I am. You'll go to prison with me. You think they will believe that I did this on my own?'"

She felt her blood run cold at Frieda's words. "Who did help him?"

Frieda shook her head. She took a ragged breath. "He never told me." Nikki could tell that she was in terrible pain. "All I cared about was the babies. I told him I was taking them and going to the authorities."

"'You're not doin' nothin' but goin' back to the ranch and keepin' your trap shut.' I told him I couldn't go back, not without the babies. 'You don't go back and you'll look guilty and I will be long gone and you can rot in prison.'"

Nikki couldn't bear to hear this and yet she

hung on every word as she prayed for the sound of the ambulance and sheriff.

"I knew he was right. No one would believe me," Frieda said, her voice getting weaker. "He walked over to the babies. He was going to put them into that grave he'd dug. Put them in there still alive. I picked up the shovel." She began to cry again. "I dug the hole larger and buried him and the ransom money."

"What did you do with the babies, Frieda?" Nikki asked, her voice breaking.

The woman's eyes met hers. "I took them to the Whitehorse Sewing Circle. Pearl Cavanaugh was the only one there that night after everyone else had gone. I told her the same story I told Harold about Marianne. I begged her to find them good homes."

Relief rushed through her. "And did she?"

Frieda didn't answer. When Nikki looked into her eyes again, she saw that the woman was gone.

Chapter Eighteen

Across the ravine, Cull saw a man with a rifle run to his pickup. Something flashed in the sunlight as the man jumped behind the wheel. A moment later he took off in a cloud of dust. Was he going for help? What had he been doing with a rifle?

Cull pulled over to the side of the road and jumped out to look down into the ravine. In the distance he could hear the sound of sirens as he looked down to the bottom and saw the wrecked rental car. His heart dropped.

"Nikki!" he called. *"Nikki!"* He had already started down the hillside at a run when she came out from behind the rocks. His mouth went dry. He hadn't realized how terrified he'd been until he saw her—saw her injured and covered in blood.

He ran to her, weak with relief. "How badly are you hurt?" He could see that she had a scrape on the side of her face and there was dried blood on her temple, but it was the blood on the front of her shirt that had him shaking inside.

"It's not me. It's Frieda." She burst into tears. "She's been shot. She's dead."

He pulled her into his arms, the sound of sirens growing closer. She felt so good in his arms that he never wanted to let her go. Relief gave way to realization. He'd seen the shooter leave in that old truck. "Did you get a look at the shooter?"

Nikki shook her head against his chest. "He ran us off the road, then came back…"

A sheriff's department patrol SUV stopped at the top of the hill followed by an ambulance, sirens blaring.

"Let's get you up to the road," he told Nikki.

She pulled back to wipe her eyes. "I can't leave Frieda."

"Let the EMTs take care of Frieda."

"But I'm the one who got her killed."

Chapter Nineteen

It rained the day of Frieda Holmes's funeral, but all of the McGraws were there standing under black umbrellas, listening to the preacher put her to rest. Frieda had no family except for the McGraws. But members of her quilting group had come to pay their respects.

Nikki stood next to Cull, the rain making a soft patter on the umbrella he held over them. Her heart still ached for Frieda. She'd paid a high price for what she'd done and the secret she'd kept all these years.

Still shaken by what had happened, Nikki questioned why she'd become a true crime writer. What drove this need of hers for the truth? Whatever it was, she'd gotten the woman killed. Her relentless need to dig in other people's tragedies had caused this. She would have to take that to her own grave.

As she looked around the cemetery, she

thought of her father. She knew now that he had nothing to do with the kidnapping, but it would take more than that to clear his name. She had to find out who inside that house had helped Harold Cline. She would never believe it was Frieda.

The preacher was winding up his sermon. She looked to Travers McGraw, wondering how he was holding up given everything that had happened. He stood tall and erect beside the cook's grave, insisting he didn't need the wheelchair. In the days since Patricia's arrest, he'd improved. No doubt because he wasn't being poisoned, but it would take time for him to recover—if he ever fully did.

Cull had been afraid that the news about the twins would be the straw that finally broke him. But Nikki saw that he was filled with even more hope now. He was also stronger now that he knew why his health had deteriorated like it had. He would never be the man he'd been, but he was more determined than ever to find the twins.

The family gathered back at the ranch after the funeral. Tilly had made them all lunch, but no one was hungry. There were still so many questions, but now at least they knew that the babies had been saved. Unfortunately, Pearl Cavanaugh, the member of the Whitehorse Sewing

Circle who Frieda had given the twins to, was dead. She'd died some years ago after having several strokes.

Travers had asked Nikki to tell them all what Frieda had confessed before she died. When she finished, the room fell silent.

"You believe Patty was poisoning our mother twenty-five years ago?" Ledger asked.

"It would explain your mother's behavior," Nikki said. "I'm not sure the sheriff will be able to prove it, though."

"We still don't know who helped this Harold Cline take the twins," Boone pointed out.

"But we do know that Frieda got them to Pearl Cavanaugh and that she probably found them good homes," Nikki said.

"But she is the only one who knows where they went and she's dead," Boone pointed out. "It's just another dead end."

"I have to wonder about the adoptive parents," Cull added. "They had to know about the McGraw kidnapping. It was on national news. Wouldn't they have questioned where their babies came from?"

Nikki had thought of that. "I'm sure Pearl had a story prepared. Remember, Frieda told her that Marianne wasn't stable, that the babies weren't safe here. I'm sure the new parents thought they were saving them."

"They were," Travers said.

"Which means they aren't together. Oakley and Jesse Rose had to have been adopted separately," Ledger said.

The room fell silent for a few moments.

"What now?" Boone asked, looking at Nikki, then his father.

"I'm sure Nikki is still planning to do the book," Travers said, and Nikki nodded. "I got a call from the sheriff earlier. They found the hunting cabin in the Little Rockies that Harold Cline used. They found his grave and the ransom money." His voice broke as he added, "The sheriff found a burlap bag in the cabin that had both Oakley's and Jesse Rose's DNA on it."

He turned to Nikki. "One of the things that was never released to the media was that when the twins were taken, so were their favorite animals that slept with them at night—and their blankets. Jesse Rose's blanket was found in the pool house. But Oakley's was never found. The small stuffed animals were horses with ribbons around their necks. Each twin had a different-colored ribbon."

Cull frowned. "So there is one blanket and two stuffed horses still missing. Let me guess. You're planning to release this information in hopes that the twins will see it."

Travers smiled at his son and nodded. "Just the information about the toy horses."

Boone got to his feet. "You're going to bring every nutcase out of the woodwork. Isn't it bad enough with all the publicity about Patricia?"

"The twins are alive," Travers said. "I've felt it soul deep since they were taken. What Nikki found out from Frieda only proves it. This is a chance I have to take. With Nikki's help, we'll put out the information and pray that the twins will find *us*."

Boone shook his head. "I have work to do. We are still a horse ranch, aren't we?" He walked out, mumbling, "This family is cursed."

"He's right. I still can't believe what Patty did," Cull said, looking over at his father.

"I suspect she got the idea from when she slowly poisoned your mother over twenty-five years ago and made her think she was crazy," Travers said.

Cull shook his head in disbelief. "She would have killed you and none of us would have suspected what she was doing. If Jim Waters gets her out of jail…"

"He won't," Travers said. "Patricia has no money of her own. She won't be able to make bail. Not only that, but also the judge thinks she is a flight risk and so do I."

"You're sure Waters isn't defending her?" Cull asked with disgust.

"He might have, before he realized she didn't have any money to pay him. Before we got married, I made Patricia sign a prenuptial agreement. I worried that if we divorced she could force me to sell the ranch that I've built for my children."

"But she would get something. What happened if you died?" Nikki asked.

"She would have gotten a few acres so she could build a place for herself, if she so desired, and a large amount of money to live on the rest of her life. I'm sure she would have sold the land," Travers said. "Now we know that she couldn't wait for me to die." There was pain in his tone. He wasn't used to being betrayed.

"Nikki tells me that your mother kept a diary," Travers said to his sons. "One of the pages has turned up. Do you know anything about it?" he asked his family. There was a general shake of heads.

"The first I heard of it was when Nikki brought me the page someone had shoved under her door," Cull said. "Isn't it possible Patricia was involved? She seems to have been involved in everything else, including blackmailing Frieda."

"I'm going to go by the sheriff's office and

see if Patty will talk to me," Nikki said. "If she has the diary hidden somewhere, I doubt she will give it up, though. But all I can do is try."

"Good luck with that," Cull piped up.

"Did the sheriff say if they've had any luck finding the person who ran us off the road and shot Frieda?" Nikki asked.

Travers shook his head. "They're looking for the pickup that both you and Cull provided a description for, but they've had no luck so far. There are so many old barns around here, not to mention thousands of ravines and ponds where it could have been dumped. That's what the sheriff thinks Frieda did with Harold Cline's old car he drove. She suspects it is rusting out in one of the ponds near the Little Rockies. It wouldn't be the first time a vehicle was hidden in one."

"Are you sure Patty wasn't in on the kidnapping?" Ledger asked.

Nikki shook her head. "Frieda didn't know who Harold Cline had helping him in the house. It could have been Patty, but I have my doubts. Yes, she wanted your mother's life, always did. The kidnapping I believe messed up her plans and forced her to leave. Also because of the large ransom demand, your father didn't have any money for a long while after that." Nikki shrugged. "It wasn't until she had her daughter and your father had recouped his losses that she doubled back."

"We still don't know who fathered her baby?" Ledger asked.

His father shook his head. "I never asked. Kitten has gone to stay with an aunt. Patricia insisted." He sounded sad. Travers had raised the child as his own and now she, too, had been taken from him.

Cull swore. "That coldhearted—"

"Patricia will get what's coming to her," Travers said as he got to his feet. "Boone's right. We have a horse ranch to run. Nikki will take care of releasing the information to the media. She tells me she can do that from back home while she's writing the book, so she'll be leaving tomorrow. Thank you again. If you hadn't come here…" He smiled at her, his eyes filling with tears.

"She can't finish her book until we find the twins," Ledger said. "So I hope that means you'll be back."

"We'll see what releasing the information about the twins' stuffed animals turns up." She glanced over at Cull. He seemed to be studying the toes of his worn boots.

Ledger rose to his feet.

"Tell me you aren't going into town to the Whitehorse Café," Cull said, finally glancing up.

His younger brother shrugged. "You've never been in love, so you couldn't possibly understand."

"Uh-huh," Cull said. "Just watch your back. I hope I don't have to warn you about Wade Pierce."

"There is nothing you can tell me about him that I don't already know," Ledger said, and headed for the door.

"You're worried about him," Nikki said when she and Cull were alone. She shared his concern.

"With good reason. My brother is in love with another man's wife. No good can come out of that." He settled his gaze on her. "So you're leaving."

"I'll go home and start the book. I can do what your father needs me to do from there. No reason for me to stay now."

"I guess not." He lumbered to his feet. "Well, if I don't see you before you leave, have a safe trip back home."

NIKKI HAD TWO things she had to do before she left town tomorrow. She had to see Marianne McGraw again and then she would pay a visit to Patricia in jail.

This time she went through proper channels, and having Travers's permission, she was taken down the long hallway to the woman's room. Nothing had changed since the last time she'd been here.

Marianne was in her rocker, the dolls clutched in her arms, her slippered feet propelling her back and forth as she stared off into space.

Nikki dragged up the extra chair in the room and sat down in front of the woman. "You probably don't remember me. I came here to find out who kidnapped your children. I promised I would come back when I knew."

There was no change in expression or in the rocking motion.

"It was your cook Frieda Holmes's boyfriend. She wasn't involved. But the news I have to tell you is that her boyfriend is dead. She killed him and saved your babies. We suspect they went to good homes and eventually we will find them. So we believe that Oakley and Jesse Rose are alive."

Still nothing.

"You should also know that twenty-five years ago when you thought you were losing your mind? You were being *poisoned*. That's why you were confused. It's why you were having trouble bonding with the twins. Patty, your nanny, was poisoning you. She wanted your husband—and she finally got him. She's in jail for attempted murder because once she had

Travers, she decided to get rid of him. Apparently what she really wanted was the ranch and you out of the way."

Marianne seemed to hug the dolls tighter as she rocked.

Nikki couldn't be sure any of this was getting through the walled-up dark place where the woman's mind had holed up all these years.

"Now everyone knows you had nothing to do with the kidnapping. Your name is cleared and soon, God willing, your twins will be found alive and well and Patty will be in her prison."

She looked into the woman's face for a moment, remembering the last time she was here. She'd gotten a reaction out of Marianne, but this time there was nothing.

Standing, Nikki pushed the chair back. "I'm so sorry you can't hear what I'm saying. I'd hoped it might free you." She turned and walked to the door to tap on it. A moment later, the door opened.

As she started to step out, she looked back, realizing that the rocking had stopped. Marianne was looking at her. Her arms opened and the tattered dolls tumbled to the floor. The woman let out a bloodcurdling cry that Nikki knew she would hear in her dreams the rest of her life.

"I CAN'T BELIEVE you'd have the nerve to come here," Patricia snapped as Nikki took the phone in the visitors' room and sat down on the safe side of the Plexiglas. "Your lies got me in here. But I'll get out. I have friends."

"I think lover more than friend," Nikki interrupted. "So which one of them were you arguing with the first night I arrived? Was it Blake Ryan or Jim Waters? I can see Kitten in either of them. I bet a DNA test would prove which one was her father. I'm also betting that whichever one it was, it was his idea for you to come back to Whitehorse and the McGraw ranch."

Patricia narrowed her eyes. "You think you know so much, don't you? Prove any of it."

"A simple DNA test will do that."

"Like I'm going to allow my daughter to be tested."

"You do realize that once the sheriff starts questioning Blake Ryan and Jim Waters, your... lover will turn on you and make a deal. Once the sheriff finds the old truck one of them used to force me and Frieda off the road... Once they find the man's DNA inside... I know he shot her to shut her up. If Travers had found out that you'd withheld information on the kidnapping... Well, he might have changed his will—before you killed him—and cut you off without a cent."

"You don't know what you're talking about."

"I know you don't want the twins to be found. You don't need two more McGraws turning up when you already have three stepsons watching you. But a little more poison and Travers's next heart attack would have probably killed him. You would have had some land to sell and money to do whatever you wanted. What did you plan to do, Patty?"

"Are you sure you aren't a fiction writer? It seems to me you just make things up as you go," the woman said. "What do you want?"

"To say goodbye. I'm leaving."

"Finally. Too bad you ever came here."

Nikki stared at her. She'd met others who lacked true compassion. Psychopaths who took pleasure in hurting others. People like Patty only felt pain when it was their own. She thought of the mousy nanny. No wonder no one had suspected what she was doing to poor Marianne. Not that the sheriff would ever be able to prove it.

"Did you ever have a dog?" Nikki asked.

"*What?* A dog? What does that have—"

"Just curious. I've found that people who can't love an animal are missing a part of their souls."

"I have no idea what you're trying to say," she said, looking away.

"I told Marianne that you were systematically poisoning her twenty-five years ago and that was why she thought she was losing her mind."

Patty laughed. "Marianne? She's a vegetable. You really can't believe she understood anything you said."

"You might be surprised." Nikki stood, still holding the phone. "By the way, what did you do with her diary?"

Was that surprise in her eyes? "Her life was so boring. Why would she bother to keep a diary?"

"Have it your way. I would imagine you'll produce it if you can find a way for it to help save you. But ultimately, you're going away for a very long time. I bet Blake is making a deal right now with the prosecuting attorney."

Patty looked scared. Nikki felt bad that she took pleasure in seeing the woman squirm. She thought of what Patty had done to Marianne, Frieda and Travers, and didn't feel so bad.

As she hung up the phone, she saw Patricia signal the guard that she was done.

Chapter Twenty

Nikki didn't see Cull when she went up to the house to say goodbye to Travers and tell him about both Marianne's and Patty's reactions to her visits.

"I'm sorry to see you go," the older man said. "You saved my life. I'll never forget that. Are sure you can't work from here?"

"This is best."

He nodded slowly. "My boys…well, they're gun-shy of relationships. Rightly so, given what they've been through. But you and Cull…"

She smiled. "There was a lot going on. I think we all need time."

"Maybe." He walked her out to her new rental car, which had been delivered that morning. "We'll talk soon."

Nikki held back the tears until she reached the ranch gate. She made the mistake of looking back. A half-dozen of the horses stood at the fence watching her leave. She thought of her father. He'd been innocent just as her mother had known, just as Nikki had prayed.

But what brought tears to her eyes was the pain in her heart. Cull had unlocked something in her. She could just hear what her grandfather would have said—if she was crazy enough to tell him.

She'd gotten too emotionally involved. With the family. With the story. With the oldest son. She and Cull had connected in a way that had scared them both. They were too young to feel this way, weren't they?

Look at Ledger. He'd fallen in love with Abby at the Whitehorse Café when they were teenagers—and nothing had changed even when she'd foolishly married another man. Nikki hoped they found their way back to each other. Ledger deserved a happy ending. So did Cull, but she figured it would be with some local girl now that the truth had come out about the kidnapping.

She drove away from the ranch, telling herself she'd be back but wondering if she ever would. Could she bear seeing Cull again? Bear seeing him with another woman? She thought not.

Tears blurred her eyes. She made a swipe at them as she drove, forcing her to slow down.

CULL WAS SADDLING his horse when his brothers found him. "What's up?" he asked, half-afraid something else had happened.

"We need to talk to you," Boone said. "What's going on between you and the writer?"

Cull almost laughed. This was it? "None of your damned business." He turned back to saddling the horse. He needed this ride more than either of them could imagine. Nikki was the only thing on his mind and he had to do something about that. He did his best thinking on the back of a horse.

"Are you serious about her?" Ledger asked.

Cull sighed and turned back to them. "Maybe I didn't make myself clear—" He frowned. "I thought you went into town?"

"Boone needed my help to make you see reason. We like Nikki. We think she's good for you," Ledger said, taking him by surprise. "She…challenges you. You need that."

Boone sighed. "You do realize that once she gets what she needs for her book she has no excuse to come back."

"I'm aware of that."

"Personally, I don't care what you do, but Ledger is convinced you're in love with her and too stupid to do anything about it."

"Thanks," he said to his youngest brother.

"Well, what *are* you going to do about it?" Ledger asked. "You going to let her get away?"

"She isn't some horse I can lasso and haul back to the corral," Cull said, annoyed that they were butting into his love life. His love life? Had he just thought that? "The woman has a mind of her own."

"So if you could lasso her and haul her back to the corral, you would?" Ledger demanded.

In a heartbeat. "I'm not discussing this with the two of you. Not one lovesick brother who lost his woman or a brother who's too ornery to ever lasso a woman."

"I don't want to see you make the mistake I did," Ledger said, obviously not taking offense at Cull's description of him.

"I could lasso any woman I want. I just haven't found one worth bringing back to the corral," Boone protested.

Cull shook his head. "What do you want from me?"

"If you love her, then go after her. Tell her how you feel," Ledger said.

"And if she leaves anyway?" he asked, hating how vulnerable he sounded.

"Then at least you tried," Boone said, surprising him even more. "We already have one brother moping around here over a woman. I can't bear two. Fix it." With that his brother turned and stalked away.

"He's right," Ledger said. "Fix it or you'll regret it the rest of your life."

"She's already gone," he said.

"You might be able to catch her if you take the shortcut across the ranch," Ledger suggested. "Since you were going on a horseback ride anyway." He smiled.

Cull cuffed his brother on the shoulder as he swung up in the saddle. "I'll think about it."

CULL RODE HARD toward the cutoff road. It felt good, the wind in his face, the power of the horse under him, the freedom of escape that filled him.

He couldn't believe that his brothers had ganged up on him. Go after Nikki and what? Tell her he didn't want her to go? Even with Patricia out of the house, things were still too up in the air.

Not only that; he also told himself that he barely knew the woman. It wasn't like he could have fallen in love with her that quickly. It wasn't like it had been love at first sight. He thought of her lying on the street in front of his pickup and groaned.

She'd never admitted that she'd done that on purpose. What kind of woman would risk her life for…for what? To make him more sympathetic to the book she planned to write?

Pretty daring thing to do. He hated the admiration he felt. It had been a stupid thing to do. Too risky. She could have been killed. A woman like that...well, who knew what she'd do next.

He smiled to himself at the thought. He'd never met anyone like her. He could see her fitting in just fine on the ranch now that Patricia was gone. He could see her just fine as his wife.

That thought hit him like a low limb.

He'd almost reached the road. In the distance he could make out her rental car. A tail of dust trailed behind it.

Cull brought his horse up short at the fence. Why had he let his brothers talk him into this? He had no idea what he was going to say to her. For all he knew she didn't feel the same way. She might even have a boyfriend back home.

Not the way she kissed you. He smiled to himself, remembering those kisses and hating the thought of never getting another one. He'd never told any woman that he loved her. He'd had crushes, even dated the same girl a couple of years in high school. He'd loved her, but he hadn't *loved* her. Not the kind of love that lasts a lifetime.

Nikki was getting closer. He could almost make out her face through the windshield.

Ride away now! You're just going to make a fool of yourself.

NIKKI COULDN'T BELIEVE what she was seeing. She squinted through the sun-dappled windshield. Was that Cull on a horse waiting for her by the ranch fence?

She touched the brakes, wondering what he wanted as she slowed and hurriedly wiped away the rest of her tears. Maybe she'd forgotten something. But he didn't seem to have anything in his hands. Or maybe Travers had sent him with a message.

Bringing the car to a stop next to him and his horse, she lowered the passenger-side window. "Is something wrong?"

Cull nodded. She watched him slide out of the saddle. He hesitated for a moment, his gaze meeting hers before he vaulted over the fence. As he walked toward her new rental car, her heart lodged in her throat. She'd fallen so desperately in love with this man. How had she let that happen?

He leaned in the passenger-side window she'd lowered.

"I've been thinking," he said, and cleared his throat. "You're going to have to get over your fear of horses."

She frowned. Surely he hadn't ridden all this way to tell her that. "Really? I suppose you have something in mind?"

Cull's blue gaze locked with hers. "I have all

kinds of things in mind." He let out a curse and drew back only to walk around to her side of the car. Opening the door, he reached for her hand.

Still mystified, she let him take it and pull her from behind the wheel. "Cull, what—"

"I don't want you to go."

"I'll be back to do more work on the book." It was a lie. She couldn't bear being this close to him and not being in his arms. She wouldn't be back.

"No," he said as if struggling to find the right words. Again his gaze met hers and held it. "I... I know it sounds crazy. It *is* crazy. I come riding out here like some kind of a fool being chased by the devil to tell you..." He faltered.

"To tell me...? Has something happened to your father?"

He shook his head. "I love you." He let out a breath and laughed. "I. *Love*. You."

She was so surprised that she didn't know what to say. She hadn't let herself admit her feelings until today. She'd blamed whatever it was between them on simple chemistry. She and Cull had been like fire and ice. But when they were fire...

"I just had to tell you how I feel." He took a step back from her. "I feel...better getting it out, how about that?" He grinned. "I think I've been wanting to say that for a while now." His blue eyes shone as they locked with hers. "I still can't believe it. I love you."

Nikki laughed. "That's it?"

He looked taken aback. "Hell, woman, you have no idea how hard that was to say. I've never told anyone…and you…you—" He blew out air as he stepped to her again. "*You* make me crazy." His fingers caught her hair at the nape of her neck and buried themselves in the long strands. "All I think about is kissing you. I want to make love to you slow and easy. I want to wake up every morning with you in my arms. I can't stop thinking about you. I don't think I can live without you."

She couldn't breathe at his words, at the look in his eyes. "Oh, Cull. From the moment I laid eyes on you… I felt…" She shook her head. "I've never felt like this before. I love you too."

He pulled her to him in a sizzling kiss that left her teetering on her high heels. As he drew back, he said, "The first thing we're going to do is buy you a pair of cowboy boots, woman."

She laughed. "*That's* the first thing?"

Cull dragged her into another kiss, this one hotter than the last. "Maybe not the first thing."

* * * * *